Henry Stewart Cunningham

The Heriots

Henry Stewart Cunningham

The Heriots

ISBN/EAN: 9783742809797

Manufactured in Europe, USA, Canada, Australia, Japa

Cover: Foto ©Andreas Hilbeck / pixelio.de

Manufactured and distributed by brebook publishing software
(www.brebook.com)

Henry Stewart Cunningham

The Heriots

BY

SIR HENRY STEWART CUNNINGHAM, K.C.I.E.

AUTHOR OF
'CHRONICLES OF DUSTYPORE,' 'WHEAT AND TARES,' 'THE CŒRULEANS,'
ETC.

IN THREE VOLUMES

VOL. III

London

MACMILLAN AND CO.

AND NEW YORK

1890

CONTENTS

CHAPTER XXXI

THE TROUBLES OF COURTSHIP

'I would that you were all to me,
  You that are just so much, no more :
  Nor yours nor mine, nor slave nor free !
  Where does the fault lie ?   What the core
  O' the wound, since wound must be ? '

DE RENZI'S courtship was not just now a bed
of roses to him.   He had begun to feel the
first chill gusts of the approaching storm.
He was feeling already the inconveniences of
an unworldly marriage—his father's cynical
disapproval, his mother's ill-concealed disappointment, his sisters' uncomplimentary
silence about their future relation, the fancied
sneers of kind friends at so interesting a
lapse into the sentimental.   Olivia's reception
by his own relations was, De Renzi felt

bitterly, a foretaste of the family discomforts which awaited his wife and himself in times to come. They froze her with politeness, which was in the circumstances the acme of discourtesy. They dared not insult her, but their behaviour breathed a subtle insolence. There was no attempt at intimacy; no pretence of the goodwill that will soon ripen into affection. Sir Raphael went his way, · Lady de Renzi and the young ladies went theirs; their thoughts were busy; their leisure was small; their days overcrowded with engagements: there seemed no space for Olivia anywhere to find a resting-place, no spot where she could strike a spark of kindness. More than once she had come back from visiting her future relations with ruffled nerves and in an agitated temper, and had expressed herself about them with an outspokenness which filled Mrs. Heriot's soul with the direst apprehensions. The case was one which baffled her powers of analysis.

She could not diagnose, she could not
prescribe for it.   Olivia's light-heartedness
appeared to be deserting her at the very
moment when joy, confidence, triumph, ought,
as she judged, to be at their highest pitch.
She had rallied Olivia sometimes on her
melancholy moods, as accidents which
naturally befall people who are excessively
in love, the mere reaction of overwrought
sentiment.   Lovers are traditionally a moody,
wayward race, who vex their own and each
other's souls with groundless alarms, unjust
suspicions, imaginary grievances.   Comfort,
tranquillity, happiness, come only with
marriage.   And what marriage could promise more happily, more auspiciously than
Olivia's ?

Once, coming suddenly into Olivia's room,
Mrs. Heriot had found her in tears.   There
was no time for concealment, nor did Olivia
attempt it.   These exhibitions of waywardness were, to Mrs. Heriot, excessively pro-

voking. They were girlish folly, of which
any rational being ought to be heartily
ashamed. They deserved rough handling—
they required it. How could the bride-elect
of one of the richest and most brilliant young
men in London have any conceivable excuse
for crying? Such moods were best combated
by a judicious firmness. 'What is the matter
now, Olivia?' she asked in a tone that
breathed anything rather than sympathy.
'Are you ill, or have you had a lovers'
quarrel? What is it you are crying about?
You will make yourself a perfect fright.'

Olivia speedily was mistress of herself.
'Was I crying?' she said. 'Well, Isabella,
perhaps it was because my new relations are
so kind to me—that is, if they ever become
my relations.'

'If ever they become!' cried Mrs. Heriot
in consternation. 'You do not mean to say,
Olivia, that you are doubting?'

'Just now,' said Olivia, 'I doubt every

thing but one, and that is that I dislike Lady
de Renzi and her daughters. I am positive
of that. I shall always dislike them; they
are not likeable.'

'Not likeable?' asked her cousin. 'I like
them well enough.'

'Possibly,' said Olivia; 'and so might
I, if I was not doomed to become their
relation.'

'Doomed!' cried Mrs. Heriot. 'What can
you possibly mean?'

'I mean,' said Olivia, 'that it is a misfortune to belong to such people as Lady de
Renzi. She is vulgar, worldly, overbearing.
As soon as I am married she will begin to
tyrannise over me. She dislikes me, and I
return the compliment.'

'How can you talk like that, Olivia, even
to me?' said Mrs. Heriot. 'Of course, if
you have thoughts like that in your mind,
Lady de Renzi will dislike you. Fortunately,
you are marrying Claude, not his mother.'

'Fortunately,' said Olivia; 'or perhaps unfortunately. Who can tell?'

'What!' cried her companion; 'do you mean that you are doubting about Claude?'

'I am doubting about everything,' said Olivia. 'I doubted when he proposed to me.' I am as doubtful now as then—doubtful whether I ought to have accepted him—doubtful if I am the right wife for him—doubtful if he loves me as he ought, or I love him as I ought—doubtful if I can ever be all he will wish for in his wife—doubtful whether I can honestly go on. Isabella, I am miserable; have mercy on me, and help me. What am I to do?'

But there was no mercy to be seen in Mrs. Heriot's cold gray eyes; rather a steady rigidness, a glance of scorn, provocation, resentment. She looked now with steady determination at Olivia; her lips were rigid, her face was like iron, her tones incisive. It was no moment, she was thinking, for hesitation or reserve. The crisis was too acute.

'Olivia,' she said, 'we had better understand each other. I will not be made a fool of; nor, if I can help it, let you make a fool of yourself. You are behaving now like a fool. I will have no such folly here. There must be no backing out of your engagement, no nonsense about your future relations : you have not got to marry them, nor need you love them or like them, though I should advise you to be as civil to them as you can. But you *have* got to marry Claude de Renzi. You have known him for two years ; you have constantly met ; you know each other thoroughly ; you have never disguised your feelings about him ; you loved him a month ago well enough to accept him ; it is nonsense to suppose that you do not love him now. Love or no love, you must go on. I will have no jilting in my house, and no playing with the idea of it, as you are doing now.

You must be out of your senses to think of it.
You know what your position is. I have
done everything for you. Thanks to me,
you are about to make a splendid match.
To throw over such a marriage for a whim—
a silly girlish caprice—would be the act of an
idiot. You must be an idiot for it even to
have occurred to you. There is not a girl in
London who does not envy you your good
luck. Remember, please, that if you break
with Claude you break with me. I shall
have nothing more to do with you. You will
have to go back to Axborough and teach
your cousins arithmetic.'

'I would sooner do that,' cried Olivia,
flushing up and looking wild and rebellious,
'than marry a man whom I am not sure of
loving. I will do it if needs be.'

'I shall be as good as my word,' said Mrs.
Heriot; 'you may rely upon that. But I
know you mean to be a good girl, and
behave like a rational being. This evening

you are overwrought and excited. We are both excited. Do not let us talk about it any more till we are cooler. I have confidence in your good sense.'

The conciliatory close of Mrs. Heriot's harangue had been inspired by Olivia's appearance. She looked like a young rebel angel of a determined order. She had it in her to rebel, it was certain; she would do so unless handled judiciously. So Mrs. Heriot felt that she had been too peremptory, too plain-spoken.

'I wish that I could share your confidence,' said Olivia, 'or that I could feel confident about anything. I wish to do what is right, Isabella; I mean to do it, cost me what it may. Only please do not drive me.'

Mrs. Heriot began to understand that Olivia, if she was to go in the desired direction, required extremely gentle driving.

CHAPTER XXXII

IT RAINS DIAMONDS

'Il y a bien peu de femmes qui n'aient entrevu le ciel a
l'heure de leurs fiançailles, et ne donneraient une partie
de leur vie pour l'entrevoir encore.'

THUS Olivia's soul was beginning to drift
apart in solitude, tempest-tossed on waves
of doubt, carried this way and that by con-
flicting currents of emotion. On the one
side the world was beaming upon her with
siren smiles. The incense of homage floated
rich and delicious around her. The world
was at her feet. If she entered a drawing-
room she knew that her presence at once
became a force that was felt; men were
continually asking to be introduced to her;
women were continually inventing excuses

to become friends with her. She had a
sense—a delightful thrilling sense—of success.
Society found her delightful, crowned her
with flowers, and led her from one triumph
to another. In a few weeks she would be
in possession of all in the way of splendour,
pleasure, importance that wealth could give.
Meanwhile her every whim was law. Claude
was always on the look-out for some new
way in which he might gratify her caprice.
He loaded her with presents. Her jewelry
had till now consisted of a few relics of her
mother's scanty store—poor little shabby bits
of finery which she had safeguarded in former
days with a religious care. Now treasures
poured in amain. Sir Raphael sent her a
diamond necklace, which no female eye—
not Olivia's certainly—could contemplate
without emotion. Claude himself was continually bringing her some new costly
offering, always in the best taste, *recherché*,
beautiful, such as a lovely woman might well

love wherewith to decorate her loveliness. Rich relations and a wide circle of those who were friends of the De Renzis, or who wished to become so, kept up the golden deluge. Olivia was pleased with her new acquisitions. They were her own; she had never owned anything worth sixpence before. The sensation was novel and agreeable. Yet in the cup of mortal enjoyment there is always the *amari aliquid.* Olivia began to get *blasée* of splendid gifts. With their novelty they lost their charm. Claude condemned not a few of them, as in bad taste, or insufficient in splendour—a blunder or an impertinence on the donor's part. They gave Claude himself, it was obvious, not the slightest satisfaction, except in so far as they gratified Olivia. Such presents as Olivia in former years had received—few, meagre, and of a cheapness that it was now almost a joke to remember— had always meant love, friendship, or sentiment. Olivia felt now with some bitterness

that many of her new acquisitions meant
nothing—nothing, that is, beyond the con-
ventional compliment due from the donor to
Sir Raphael de Renzi for business favours,
or to his wife for a given number of
dinners, balls, and other social favours.

'Look at this amethyst cross,' she said to
Claude one morning; 'is it not lovely?
Who is Lady Everard? Why has she sent
it to me, I wonder?'

'Do you?' De Renzi answered. 'There
is nothing to wonder at. It is gratitude in
its purest form, a keen sense of favours to
come. Her husband wants my father's sup-
port in a railway which he is wanting to run
through his side of the county. It is to go
right through his estate, and will be worth,
I daresay, £100,000 to him. That cross is
worth perhaps £50—no!—there is a flaw in
that amethyst—it is not worth £30. It is
not a bad investment, is it, of Lady Everard?
Let us hope it will pay.'

How to find satisfaction in presents so given? in base offerings to court the favour of a millionaire, to buy profitable influence— as much a part of speculative outlay as the cost of advertisements or the commission of an agent. When Olivia's home was broken up, some village children, whom she loved, had clubbed their halfpennies together and bought of a pedlar, who represented to them the fine arts and commerce of the outer world, a pincushion of hideous splendour, which they presented with much ceremony and soul-stirring emotion to the dear friend who was passing out of their horizon for ever. It could not, on the most generous calculation, have been worth a shilling; but Olivia had received it with tears, with a throbbing heart, with painful pleasure; she remembered it with a glow of affection. None of her splendid marriage offerings had ever stirred a single one of the emotions which lay, thick as the leaves in Vallombrosa, carpeting the untrodden solitude of her existence. They lay there—but no gust of sentiment disturbed them. Her lover's presents were almost as bad as the rest. They were given with prosaic indifference; they lacked romance. They were less the outpouring of a generous soul than judicious investments for one who, by formal arrangements, was to become a member, a brilliant member, of the De Renzi family. Claude haggled over the price of his purchases, drove excellent bargains, and would not buy unless the price was such as satisfied him that he was getting his money's worth. A lover's gift, Olivia romantically deemed, ought not to be too carefully appraised by the giver.

Now again, Olivia had a present which touched her. Jack Heriot called one day at his uncle's and made an excuse to speak a word to her apart. 'Come and show me your presents, Olivia. I hear they are magnificent.'

'Come,' said Olivia, leading the way to a back drawing-room where these treasures were arranged, 'but never mind the presents. I am tired to death of them. Sit down here and let us have a chat. How are they all at Huntsham? Why do you never come near me?'

'Because I am too busy, and you are too gay, Olivia. Our lives have drifted apart. We can do each other no good.'

'Indeed,' said Olivia, 'you could do me a great deal of good. I never needed my old friends so badly, or cared more for them. And you are my oldest friend, though sometimes I think you have forgotten it.'

'I shall never forget it,' cried Jack; 'I never could. What have I that I care to remember but our happy Huntsham days? Golden days they were for me. No, Olivia, whatever else I am guilty of towards you it will not be forgetfulness. But I must present my offering — a little sketch of

Huntsham, my first performance as a land-
scape painter. Some day, when I have
become famous, it will be invaluable; meanwhile it will recall the days when we were
boy and girl.'

'Those happy days!' said Olivia with a
sigh. 'What a pity that we cannot live
them over again! Thank you, Jack, for
your present. It is the one I like best
of all. But there is my cousin calling me;
I must go back to them.'

Jack went away with a full heart. Olivia
had never looked more lovely — gentler,
sweeter, more the ideal of his boyish
worship. Had her eyes been swimming
with tears when she smiled him her farewell? Jack scarcely knew, for his own
eyes had been dim. He had been in a
sort of dream. Those few moments had
translated him to Paradise, only to be
thrust out again all too soon on a cold,
loveless world. They had been a revelation.

Olivia was the same as ever. He was the same. Nature intended them for each other. Had he been a fool or poltroon to let the accidents of fortune deprive him of his rights—to let another win her? It was too late, alas, for such self-questionings to serve any purpose but to enhance the misery of frustrated hopes and vain regrets. Jack was sure now, if never before, that Olivia was his only chance of happiness, and that his loss was irremediable.

Such a scene did not aid in reconciling Olivia to her lot, her present surroundings, her new relations, her destined life. The talk with Jack recalled to her with vividness some things which she was schooling herself to forget — some canons of taste which had now to be ignored, some standards of refinement of which many things and persons around her fell short. The more she saw of her new relations the less congenial did they seem, the less prospect

was there of any future affection. Olivia
had heard nothing, at the time, of the family
opposition to her engagement. But now
the secret escaped. Claude, when she
questioned him about it, was constrained
to acknowledge that his father had not, at
first, regarded the proposed alliance with
satisfaction. 'There was nothing in that,
surely,' he protested laughingly. 'Fathers
always do—do they not?—object to a disinterested love-match like ours. I have no
doubt that he still thinks us a couple of
simpletons. That need not make us unhappy, Olivia. We are a happy pair of
lovers, are we not?'

'Most happy,' said Olivia, whose bad
spirits took immediate flight at the first
note of affection; 'I am happy, at any rate
— too happy to be disturbed by small
troubles. All the same, I wish I did not
find my relations, that are to be, quite so
terribly alarming! Lady de Renzi and your

sisters make me feel shyer than I have ever
felt before.'

'You shy!' cried De Renzi; 'but your
shyness gives the finishing touch to your
perfection ; it is the crowning charm.'

Despite her good resolutions and Claude's
encouragement, Olivia's intercourse with the
De Renzis proved, as familiarity wore off
the fine edge of politeness, increasingly
disagreeable. Their behaviour was dry, off-
hand, sometimes on the verge of rudeness.
It chilled her to the very soul. Old cam-
paigners, who have fought their way through
the world and know its rough give-and-take,
become accustomed to rudeness and indiffer-
ent to it. But to the novice—the sensitive,
gentle, ardent nature longing for sympathy,
for affection, for encouragement—unkindness
is the death-blow to high spirits. Olivia, on
the days when she went to lunch with the
De Renzis, used to come back dreadfully
depressed. They filled her with misgivings.

They emphasised the phase of Claude's character of which she had seen least, a phase of worldliness, scheming, pushing. In Lady de Renzi and her daughters it was undisguised. Did it exist in Claude? He was ambitious, of course, but ambitious in the right way, the way of noble minds— ambitious of greatness, of power; but did he also share the lower ambitions that swayed his family? Olivia's heart answered this question in a delightfully satisfactory manner. 'If he were thus ambitious — ambitious in a mean sense—would he ever have wished to marry me?' Comforting, reassuring, delightful reasoning. Claude himself made light of his relations' behaviour, and explained it with laughing apologies. 'My father,' he said, 'has been all his life coining money till he can hardly see over his gold piles. He would wish his son to follow in his wake, and begin with a lucrative marriage. I believe he thinks it is what

marriages were made for. As for my
mother, she is like other good mothers,
and I daresay had some nice little project—a
golden one—for a favourite son. We must
propitiate her.'

'Propitiate her!' cried Olivia, whose
spirits had been sinking to zero as Claude
proceeded with the family portraiture; 'I
only wish I could. But how?'

'By succeeding, dear Olivia, as you will;
by dazzling the parental vision with something better even than gold; by being, as
you cannot help being, the most beautiful,
the most brilliant, the gayest, sweetest, most
enchanting young lady of your day. You
can do it, Olivia ; you shall do it. I can see
you accomplishing it.'

'And suppose,' said Olivia, 'that I fail?
I very likely shall.'

'Fail!' cried De Renzi; 'my wife fail!
my beautiful Olivia—with all her charms,
backed by her wits and her husband's—fail!

What a conception! No, Olivia, you will succeed; all men's hearts will be yours, to say nothing of your husband's:

"Not once nor twice in polished London's story
    The path of Beauty's been the road to glory."

You will play your part to perfection.'

'Stop, stop!' cried Olivia. 'I believe that it is the right thing for lovers to be extravagant. How much am I to believe of all this? It is too much, too much. If you love me, Claude, if you are sure that you love me, it is enough.'

'If I love you!' cried De Renzi, by this time roused to excitement. 'Don't you see that I am fanatically in love with you? Am I sure indeed!'

'Well,' said Olivia, 'promise one thing, Claude. If ever you cease to be sure, will you promise to tell me? If you should ever, in the months which are to pass before our marriage, feel a doubt whether I shall be all to you that you wish your wife to be (such things happen to men, you know, sometimes), I bind you by a vow to tell me, so that I may make you free.'

'I vow,' cried De Renzi, 'that, if ever I cease to think you the most enchanting of women, I will dub myself fool, villain, and blockhead. But no, Olivia, I am yours for life and death ; you must never doubt it.'

'I will not doubt it ; I do not. I am yours, too, Claude, for life and death,' Olivia said, putting her hand in De Renzi's with a grave, tender gesture, and letting it stay there. 'Perhaps I am frightened at my own good fortune ; but I will be frightened no more.'

De Renzi's rhapsodies did not suffice to enable Olivia to regard her new relations with equanimity. She was to find no love, it was clear, among them. Her chance of being tolerated depended on her success. Olivia felt herself well qualified to succeed ;

but this use of success filled her soul with apprehension and melancholy. Had this family, of which she was about to become a member, really no hearts? Had they never known the touch of human love, the touch that makes the whole world kin? Did they know what it meant—what tenderness, sympathy, devotion meant? Sometimes in their society she had felt as if she were in pandemonium; everything was so bright, so hard, so cynical, so wanting in compassion, so unstirred by any tender or generous impulse. And it was among these people that she was for the future to find her home.

CHAPTER XXXIII

MR. COSMO'S PICNIC

'Strange and piteous to think what a centre of wretchedness
a delicate piece of human flesh might be, wrapped round
with fine raiment, her ears pierced with gems, her head
held loftily, her mouth all smiling patience, the poor
soul within her sitting in sick distaste of all things.'

ONE of the occasions on which De Renzi
wished and expected Olivia to shine was not
long in arriving. Mr. Cosmo, despite his
cynical conviction that life is not worth living,
possessed several important contrivances for
enhancing its material enjoyments. He had
a villa on the Thames, where luxury as a
fine art attained its choicest perfection, and a
steam-launch, which was no unworthy pendant
to the villa. Both were as near perfection as

Cosmo's taste and purse could make them ;
and this, the most exacting connoisseurs admitted, was very near indeed. A youth spent
in Italy had taught Cosmo the sort of abode
in which a sultry day, which scorches the outside world, may be safely defied from amid
shady recesses and cool arcades; where
fountains, plashing on the marble, offer a
delicious freshness and lull the senses to a
pleasant languor ; where everything breathes
of indolence and invites to effortless enjoyment. To this agreeable residence it was
Cosmo's custom, as the summer's heat came
on and London air became oppressive, to
invite successive parties of his friends to
spend a Sunday with him in the country.
For the occasion on which the Heriots and
Olivia, and of course, Olivia's lover, were
invited, it was arranged that the party should
steam a few miles up the river to a lovely
spot where they would find luncheon in the
shade awaiting them. This *al fresco* lunch

was a tribute to the sultry weather. Those who knew Cosmo looked forward to it with interest, for his *chef* was renowned for brilliant effects and would be sure to contrive something worthy of an inspiring occasion ; and the occasion would be inspiring, for the Duke of Egeria was to be among the guests, and several of the most agreeable men and brilliant women in London had been invited to amuse the Duke of Egeria.

De Renzi, Olivia saw, was extremely gratified at the invitation. The party, Mr. Cosmo wrote kindly, was in honour of Olivia. Mrs. Heriot, too, was delighted. Olivia found it difficult to share their enthusiasm. 'I think I dislike Sunday expeditions,' she said ; 'they make Sunday the hardest day's work of the week, and one is in sore need of a rest ; and, besides, I am a Puritan, a Methodist. I am fond of an old-fashioned Puritan Sunday.'

'I hope,' said De Renzi, on whose good

nature Olivia's announcements of this sort always had rather an irritating effect, 'that you will be able to leave the Puritan at home on this occasion, as Puritanism is not exactly what is in request at Cosmo's entertainments. People go into the country, do they not, because London Sundays are so detestably Puritanic? This party, moreover, Olivia, is intended in your honour. It is a compliment. Cosmo's parties are great events. All the smartest people in London are asked in the course of the summer. Moreover, I particularly want you to be civil to him.'

'Do you?' said Olivia. 'I will do my best; but I do not *feel* particularly civil to him; and he is too civil to me to be quite agreeable. However, I will be as polite as I can. All the same, Claude, I wish that we could get off. I feel as if I would give anything for a quiet day, a quiet evening. When was the last we had, Isabella? I believe I am very tired.'

'What nonsense!' cried Mrs. Heriot. 'It will be the best way of resting. You cannot possibly get off, and why should you?'

'Get off!' exclaimed De Renzi with a clear decisiveness which Olivia began now to observe in him whenever his will was thwarted; 'when I tell you that it is the party of all others that I want you to go to, and that I have a special reason for being glad that you are invited. What an idea!'

Olivia said nothing. She resigned herself to her fate. She had, in fact, besides her fatigue, a special reason for wishing not to go, which she did not choose to produce in public. The day in question was a sad one to her, the date of her mother's death. She and her father had always kept it with a pious observance. Little had been said or done, but each had known what was passing in the other's mind. They had kept it together for the last time, as it had proved, the summer before his death. The next time Olivia had been among strangers at the Pines and had observed it in privacy. Now it seemed a sort of pious duty to father as well as mother to keep it. Olivia longed to do so. She longed to be quiet, to be alone, to commune in spirit with the loved ones whom she had lost, to give herself to serious thoughts, which all around her ignored, which all things tended to obliterate in herself. There seemed no one to whom she dared to confide her wish. It would have been folly, profanation, to drag such a feeling out for Isabella's cold unfeeling eye to stare at. It was Olivia's secret, her own private sentiment. It was sacred to her. She dreaded profaning it. Afterwards, when they were alone together, and De Renzi seemed in a congenial mood, she told him. Alas! she was grievously disappointed at the reception that her confidence encountered. De Renzi seemed annoyed at a further attempt to controvert his wish. He evidently could not understand

her feeling.   He could not conceal that the
excuse seemed to him an absurd one.   He
was entirely unsympathetic.   Olivia, greatly
disconcerted, felt only a passionate desire to
withdraw the topic from discussion.   She
would go anywhere, she would submit to
anything rather than have the subject discussed by those who could not understand it.
'Say no more, Claude,' she said.   'I will go.
I see you wish it.   I daresay that I shall
enjoy it.   The truth is, that I have a prejudice
against Mr. Cosmo.   I cannot bear his eyes.'

'A woman's reason!' cried De Renzi,
mollified by Olivia's acquiescence.   'What do
his eyes signify to us?   They are not the
most ingenuous in the world, I admit ; nor is
candour Cosmo's forte.   None the less, his
parties are excellent.   Everybody goes to
them, or would like to go.'

'What a dreadful person Everybody is,'
said Olivia with a sigh, 'and what a tyrant
about tastes—and what odd tastes they some-

times are! Why is Everybody always to be dictating to us? For my part, I retain my opinion of Mr. Cosmo's eyes; they are detestable.'

'Well,' said De Renzi with some peremptoriness of tone, 'you have decided to go to his party, and I have given in about his eyes, so we have no points of difference. I hope you will be gracious to him.'

Mr. Cosmo was a power in the City: he controlled the policy of the great Inter-oceanic Trust, and the influence of the Inter-oceanic Trust was, just now, of importance to the De Renzis. They had a big transaction on hand, a Bolivian loan, involving vast interests to all concerned. There were rivals in the field. Opinions were divided. To lose an ally at such a moment would be disastrous. Cosmo had not yet been gained; he might be lost. To offend him would be calamitous. The essential thing was to conciliate him, and Olivia's graces were a powerful means of

conciliation. Nor was he, to all appearance,
difficult to conciliate. He was a man of
foibles, and his pet foible was to be smiled
upon by the reigning beauties of the day.
No one in certain circles, it was said, had
established her position as a woman of fashion
till she had been fêted by Cosmo. For men
he cared little, and took but little trouble to
be polite to them.

'Why are you not friends with Cosmo?'
some one had asked of Stonehouse, àpropos
of this very party.

'Because,' said that gentleman with laconic
severity, 'I do not happen to be young, pretty,
and somebody else's wife; and, moreover,
because Cosmo always reminds me of that
wise dictum of somebody's, that human nature
is a damned rascal.'

'What do you think of him yourself?'
Olivia had asked De Renzi.

'What do I think of him?' her lover
answered in the airy manner which, Olivia

knew, meant that the subject did not require further discussion; 'I think he is what he looks—estimable, benevolent, a cultured gentleman, an eminent Christian, a perfect host. In other words, Sir Raphael de Renzi and Company need his assistance for their Bolivian loan.'

'And it is for that,' cried Olivia, 'that you wish me to be gracious to him, and to endure his politeness, or, as I regard it, his impertinence? What a use to make of one!'

'Is not that a rather rough way of putting it?' pleaded De Renzi. 'Come, Olivia, come down from your sublimities and talk like a reasonable woman. We business people have our concerns to manage, like the rest of mankind. They depend on negotiation, and negotiations depend on good humour, and no one can manufacture good humour like a charming woman. It is charming woman's celestial function in a world of blundering

men. How would anything get on without
her and her benign intervention ? Into what
pie does she not dip her pretty finger-tips ?
Women move the world, they smooth irritation, they allay suspicion, they conciliate
goodwill, they supply a motive to men who
would otherwise be motiveless ; they——'

'They float Bolivian loans !' said Olivia ;
' I see. I understand it all now. We are the
light artillery in the battle of life ; we rush in
where men are afraid to tread. We effect
what men are too clumsy to manage ; we are
the chimney-sweeps whom cruel masters send
up into the soot in order not to have to go
themselves. What a grand idea of woman's
position in the world !'

'Grand or not,' said De Renzi with some
irritation, for Olivia's satirical and contempt-
uous moods seemed to him disagreeably easy
to arouse, ' it is the truth. They all do it,
and the sanctimonious ones the worst. Show
me the woman, who has the power to influence

mankind, who does not turn her powers to good account.'

'In short,' said Olivia, 'I am to bury my prejudices against Mr. Cosmo full forty fathoms deep and behave to him like an angel. Those are my orders.'

De Renzi was exceedingly provoked, but it would not do, he felt clearly, to show provocation. 'You are making too much of it altogether,' he said. 'A man, whom everybody likes and to whom everybody goes, asks you among the rest. He is powerful, and we want his power on my father's side, and not against him. What is there in our accepting his hospitality? Are we to insult him because we don't consider his manner perfect, and have a lurking suspicion that he is not a paragon of virtue? How many men are?'

'I know one man who is,' said Olivia; 'one is enough for me. Seriously, Claude, I will do exactly what you wish. I will go to the picnic. I will go anywhere you tell me.

I trust myself to you. Wherever I go, I shall feel safe so long as you are at hand to protect me.'

'You will need no protection,' said De Renzi. 'Every one acknowledges that, whatever his other shortcomings, Cosmo is a perfect host.'

'Is he?' said Olivia. 'I will take your word for it, Claude. We will discuss him no more.'

De Renzi had by this time begun to perceive that Olivia had much to learn, that she was not particularly docile, and was likely to give a great deal of trouble before her education was complete. He had an uncomfortable consciousness that he had to do with a courageous spirit, to whom fear was unknown, and whose submission would be difficult to achieve. It would be difficult to dominate such a woman. All the more resolvedly did he determine on domination.

Mrs. Heriot, too, considered that Olivia

stood in need of a little good advice. She took an early opportunity of giving her a lecture on the behaviour of a properly conducted *fiancée*.

'Do you know,' she said, 'that you are an alarmingly independent young lady, and too fastidious for a fallen world? You are endangering your own happiness. Claude is devoted to you, and will stand a great deal; but nothing shocks a man so much as self-will.'

'Self-will!' cried Olivia; 'I thought I was submissiveness itself. I did all that Claude asked me.'

'Yes,' said the other, 'but after a sort of pitched battle. Put fights of that kind off, let me advise you, Olivia, till after your marriage, and do not turn up your nose at parties which your future lord and master wishes you to grace. For my part, I cannot conceive why you should not like Mr. Cosmo.'

'Like him!' cried Olivia; 'like eyes of

blue steel, cold, cruel, hard! the smile of
Judas, the sneer of Mephistopheles.   No,
Isabella, I do not like him, nor ever shall.
He frightens, he shocks me.   I breathe more
comfortably when he is away.   I shall feel
better when this horrid party is over.   I owe
Sir Raphael de Renzi a grudge that I am
obliged to go to it.'

Olivia felt herself, her better self, her
sentiment, her tenderness, her aspirations,
being gradually asphyxiated.   In the Finnish
epic there is a story of a divine artificer who
fashions for some amorous deity a bride of
gold and silver.   The amorous deity is
pleased at first with the splendour of his new
possession; but joy gives way to horror when
he discovers that, in spite of fur and fire,
whenever he touches her she freezes him.
So Olivia, amid the glamour of wealth and
much external finery that dazzled her, began
to feel a mortal chill.   Something in her
lover was turning her to ice.   Supposing

that, like the Finnish bride, he was composed
of precious metals, not of warm and living
flesh and blood!   Olivia was running the
round of pleasure : life was one long banquet ;
but dissatisfaction, weariness of heart, *ennui*
attended at the profuse repast.   She lived in
a crowd, but, ah, how solitary may the soul
become, crowded and hustled by uncongenial
surroundings !   ' Little do men perceive,' says
Bacon, 'what solitude is, how far it extendeth.
For a crowd is not company, and faces are
but a gallery of pictures, and talk but a tink-
ling cymbal, where there is no love.'   Of this
sort of cruel, loveless solitude Olivia's gentle
soul was now becoming painfully aware.

CHAPTER XXXIV

A SUNDAY ON THE THAMES

'A bolt is shot back somewhere in our breast,
And a lost pulse of feeling stirs again ;
The eyes sink inward and the heart lies plain,
And what we mean we say, and what we would we
    know ;
A man becomes aware of his life's flow,
And hears its winding murmur ; and he sees
The meadows where it glides, the sun, the breeze ;
    And then he thinks he knows
    The hills where his hope rose
    And the sea where it goes.'

THE morning was sultry, and Mr. Cosmo's guests, as the launch went speeding amid meadow and woodland, congratulated themselves heartily on their escape from the dust and glare of London to the shade and the cool breezes that were ruffling the Thames beneath the Clifden woods. A midsummer sky blazed overhead, but cloudlets here and there spoke of disturbances in the upper regions ; and there was a heaviness in the atmosphere which seemed as if exhausted nature were panting for the refreshment of a storm. The storm, however, would not, the weatherwise predicted, be till to-morrow ; and meanwhile the languor of the outer world seemed to suggest complete self-surrender to the most indolent possible form of enjoyment. Lounging on the sofas of Cosmo's launch, with the prospect of further lounging in the delicious shade of the lime trees, beneath which the banquet of the afternoon was awaiting them, was just the sort of existence for which the party felt disposed. Everything around them spoke of pleasurable ease. The river was gay with holiday-makers, bent, like themselves, on an otiose Sunday. They passed group after group, whose merry sounds, holiday costumes, and reposeful attitudes told a pleasant tale of

ease and mirth. No one, surely, has really
seen England, or gauged the capacity of
Englishmen for play as well as work, who
has not watched the gay array of holiday-
makers who crowd the pleasant reaches of
the Thames on a fine summer day. On
either side the country lay smiling—a dream
of rest. The hay fields, still new from the
scythe, gleamed bright and clean ; great
breadths of corn were yellowing for the
harvest. The villages peeped out amid the
woodlands, the church bells were sounding
pleasantly across the meadows. The party
on the launch grew gay. The Duke of
Egeria had arrived in high spirits, evidently
resolved to enjoy himself. Every surrounding circumstance seemed to abet him in that
laudable resolution. The ladies, scattered
in picturesque groups about the sofas and
easy-chairs with which the launch abounded,
formed a charming centre to the loveliness
of surrounding nature.

Mrs. Backhouse, not too broken-hearted to be exquisitely dressed, shone serenely in a costume the artless simplicity of which all felt to be consummate art. Beside her sat Florian, whose recent volume of sonnets proclaimed the apostle of æstheticism. He was now, with the privileged outspokenness of friendship, complimenting Mrs. Backhouse on the poetry of her dress. 'It is a pastoral symphony,' he said ; 'a medley of exquisite tints. It breathes of the daffodils, the buttercups, and the daisies.'

'We will go and gather some this afternoon,' Mrs. Backhouse said, raising her lovely azure eyes to reward Florian's politeness. 'I shall expect an impromptu sonnet under the lime trees.'

There were other ladies, however, whose dresses had been designed with other ideas than that of simplicity. Miss Bond, the last imported American heiress, was as impressive in daring effects as M. Worth could make her. She was now entertaining the duke with an exhibition of naïve impertinence, which English society had been for several weeks past encouraging her to mistake for wit. The duke showed no intention of undeceiving her. Mrs. Calverby, a brilliant daughter of the Manchester plutocracy and one of Cosmo's most recent conquests, rivalled the American beauty in daring of toilette and originality of talk. There was little likelihood of conversation running short ; but, to guard against the possibility, M. Duc, the famous Sociétaire of the Comédie Française, was to give an impromptu ; and a young gentleman, known to his friends as Dodo—a spoilt darling of the Household Brigade, and one of Mrs. Backhouse's most favoured devotees—had brought his banjo, and promised to enliven the afternoon with a comic performance. The feminine ranks were further reinforced by Mrs. Mountjoy, a professional beauty, and

Mrs. Araby, a certificated wit. All seemed
perfectly familiar with each other, and all
completely at their ease—all, that is, except
Olivia, who was feeling, each moment, more
exquisitely uncomfortable. Mrs. Araby had
scanned her through her eyeglass as she
came on board, and had turned to ask something of the gentleman beside her; then she
had said something in low tones which had
produced a laugh. Miss Bond made no
secret of her satisfaction in being introduced
to Olivia, as one of the sights of London.
' I have so often heard about you,' she said
good - naturedly, 'and your gay deceiver.
Now, happily for womankind, he will deceive
no more!' Then there was another laugh,
and everybody seemed to be amused. De
Renzi did not share the amusement. He
stood frowning, and biting his moustache,
as was his custom when annoyed. Olivia
began to wish herself anywhere but where
she was. What was there to be amused at

in a vulgar American's familiarity? There
is no more effectual estrangement than a
difference of taste in jokes. Olivia felt this
estrangement; her spirits began to sink. In
vain De Renzi brought up one gentleman
after another to be introduced to her; in
vain Cosmo came and devoted himself to
being agreeable; in vain Mrs. Heriot took
her to sit by Mrs. Araby, 'the most amusing
woman in London, you know;' in vain
Dodo tried all his powers of fascination to
win her to a congenial mood; in vain was
it that Florian told a series of admir-
able stories, which sent his audience into
paroxysms of hilarity; vain were the witticisms, professional and amateur, that flashed
around; vain were Olivia's own endeavours
to be amused, to be as gay as her companions, to join in the talk that was flowing,
so brisk and bright, on all hands around her.
Her soul was growing cold within her.
Struggle against it as she would, shyness

such as she had never before experienced,
beset her, benumbing every faculty, paralys-
ing every effort at cheerfulness.   There was
something in these people, in their style,
their behaviour, their talk, their freemasonry,
which made Olivia feel herself in a world of
strangers, of enemies.   She was not neglected,
indeed ; but how grateful she would have
felt for a little kindly neglect, for assured
protection from Mrs. Araby's cynical smile,
Cosmo's eye, Miss Bond's impertinent
tongue !   She moved away and sought such
refuge as was to be found in the narrow
limits of the launch beside Mrs. Pygmalion.
Mrs. Araby presently formed a little group
around her of people with whom she could
feel sure of amusing herself.   Olivia was out
of the talk, but fragments of the conversation
fell, now and then, on her ear and obliged
her to listen.

'I have brought a book,' Mrs. Araby said,
showing a little volume to Mr. Pygmalion.

' I always do on these occasions. You never
know what may happen. If we are shipwrecked on a desert island, and food and
conversation fail, I sit secure. I am provided against the worst. Stevenson is always
delightful.'

'Delightful!' cried Pygmalion, who had
been glancing at the book's contents; 'here,
for instance, are some delightful things about
marriage! I must read you them. He de-
scribes it as a terrible renunciation!'

'Renunciation!' cried Mrs. Araby. 'Mr.
de Renzi, this is interesting to you. Pray go
on, Mr. Pygmalion.'

'"A field of battle, not a bed of roses,"'
continued Pygmalion, picking out the phrases
for public edification. '"A married man
must roam no longer. Once married, there
are no more by-path meadows where you
may innocently linger; but the road lies long,
and straight, and dusty to the grave. . . .
You may think you had a conscience and

believed in God ; but what is a conscience to
a wife ? To marry is to domesticate the
recording angel. Once you are married there
is nothing left for you, not even suicide, but
to be good." '

'What a conception of a wife!' cried Mrs.
Araby ; 'a domesticated recording angel! the
last sort of person one would wish to have
about the premises!'

'Horrible!' cried Pygmalion. 'I thought
that the great point about a wife was, that
there should be one person, at any rate, who
is firmly convinced that there is nothing to
record, or who, if there is, will drop a tear
upon the place for the purpose of effacement.'

'That is what nature intends,' said the
duke ; 'men must work, except a few of us
whose doom it is to play, and women must
weep. Poor women!'

'Of course,' cried Florian ; 'tears are her
weapon, her grand resource. Even Napoleon,
with a chaos of crushed empires at his im-

perial foot, admitted that he was no match for Josephine when she began to whimper. A tear is unanswerable.'

'The only answer, I suppose,' said Pygmalion, 'is to kiss it away.'

'In other words,' said Mrs. Araby, 'unconditional surrender.'

'And all done by a gland,' said Florian. ' So like Nature's grand simplicity—the entire male creation subjugated by a single pearly drop, which the female eye produces at its own sweet will.'

'Yes,' said Pygmalion, 'you know De Renzi's classic lines—

" When lovely woman finds 'tis folly
    To hope that husbands will obey,
 What charm will cure her melancholy,
    What art restore her threatened sway?

" The art her empire to recover,
    To quell the would-be rebel's eye ;
 To tame a disobedient lover,
    Or crush a husband—is to cry ! " ' '

'And pray,' said Mrs. Araby, turning to De Renzi, 'how did you learn that? by experience, I suppose.'

There was a general laugh; some eyes were turned on Mrs. Backhouse, some on De Renzi. Olivia happened to look up in the direction of Mrs. Backhouse, and witnessed an unusual spectacle. That lady was accomplishing a most pronounced blush—deep, prolonged, unmistakable. She looked as uncomfortable as Olivia felt.

'Spare him,' said Florian; 'he is about to domesticate his recording angel. There is nothing left to him, not even suicide, but to be good.'

'Well,' said Mrs. Araby, 'it is never too late to mend; and nowadays almost anything can be mended, however small the little bits.'

De Renzi was looking black as thunder. 'Mrs. Araby's acid drops will help the process,' he said; 'her dark innuendoes and her bright example!'

' He has *me* on his conscience,' said Miss
Bond ; 'the victim of systematic neglect.
My heart is broken.   I shall weep a small
Niagara when I get home to-night!'

' Woman's tears!' said Mrs. Araby ; ' why
is it that marriage should involve so many of
them ?'

' Because,' said the duke, ' the domesticated
angel is apt to be a little too domestic.'

'And naturally,' put in Florian, 'a little
too angelic.'

' Or,' said Cosmo, ' because, as some one
has observed, there is all the difference between being in love with a woman and being
harnessed to her—bit, blinkers, bearing rein,
and the coachman's whip if you begin to
fidget!   It is slavery, and a man hates his
slave-driver.   There must, I suppose, be
husbands and wives ; but it is inevitable that
they should be mutually disagreeable.   The
worst thing to do with a charming woman is
to marry her.'

'You remember,' said M. Duc, 'the philosophy of a countryman of mine—"Si
j'aimais une femme je la marierais peut-être,
mais pas avec moi."'

'Marriage is a mistake, no doubt,' said
Mrs. Araby; 'the great thing is to retrieve
it judiciously. To quote another of your
countrymen, M. Duc—"Ce ne sont pas
toujours nos fautes qui nous perdent; c'est la
manière de se conduire après les avoir faites."'

'But some men actually like it,' said
Cosmo. 'Rousseau, you remember, says
that he lived as happily with his Theresa—
mean, greedy, jealous, and dull—as though
she were a paragon of beauty and wit.'

'But Rousseau,' said Mrs. Araby, 'was a
genius. Moreover, he did his own recording
angel's business for himself.'

'Yes,' said Cosmo, 'and some women like
it, or behave as if they did, which encourages
the rest, happily for the world. Marriage
keeps them busy——'

'And keeps them smart,' said Florian.
' Their lovely dresses are a compliment to us.
Your earnest woman, who scorns mankind
and lives for a purpose, is apt to neglect
woman's first great purpose—her toilette.'

' I don't see that at all,' said Mrs. Backhouse ; 'the better I am dressed the better I
feel, and the more in earnest. I always put
on something pretty when I visit my hos-
pital.'

' Well,' said the duke, 'every woman
should have an object.'

' But no woman should *be* one,' said
Cosmo. ' See, here is our landing-place.'

CHAPTER XXXV

A BLACK CLOUD WITH A SILVER LINING

' As angels in some brighter dreams
  Call to the soul when man doth sleep,
So some strange thoughts transcend our wonted themes
  And into glory peep.'

THE party was soon on shore. A gentle slope of turf, stretching far on either side, formed a natural fringe to the woodland, which crept down toward the river bank. Some skilful hand had thinned the forest to the extent best calculated to reveal its charms. Here a noble stem stood out and met the eye in bold outline and relief; here a mass of creepers, tossed in romantic confusion from branch to branch, hid everything but their own fantastic exuberance; here well-shaded

avenues, cut into the wood, cool with overhanging foliage and grassy path, hinted of
pleasant depths of gloom beyond the reach
of the blazing, scorching world outside.
Every one hurried to the shade.

'Here!' cried Mrs. Backhouse, who had
no intention of letting Florian off his engagement as her cavalier; 'here we shall find the
daffodils and the daisies.   I should like to
wander all day in these delicious glades.'

'Idyllic!' cried Florian, 'with an interval,
however, for refreshments.'

'Well,' said Cosmo, 'you can have a forest
stroll now, if you prefer it to driving.   The
carriages must go round; but if you are not
afraid of a mile in the shade, we will make a
short-cut through the woodland to our lunch.
The trees are worth looking at.'

'I vote for walking!' cried Mrs. Araby, and
everybody followed her example.

'Come, Mrs. Calverby,' said Cosmo, 'let
us lead the way.'

' Who, pray,' asked the duke of Florian as they fell enough behind to be out of hearing, ' is Mrs. Calverby? I have seen her several times of late. A showy woman, finely dressed, and with fine diamonds.'

' The wife of some Stock Exchange potentate,' said Pygmalion, ' who, no doubt, gives her as many fine dresses and diamonds as she wants.'

' The City woman,' said Florian, ' or, rather, the West End woman with a City husband,

"bears
The cost of princes on unworthy shoulders." '

' Hardly on her shoulders,' said Pygmalion; ' the tide of Mrs. Calverby's extravagance does not swell quite as high as that. But, bare as they generally are, her shoulders are worthy of adoration. I must have them for my Nausicaa.'

' Why is it,' said the duke, ' that some women cultivate propriety by trying to look as improper as they can? '

'As if,' said Florian, 'they imagined
"meretricious" to be the feminine of "meri-
torious"—which, for aught I know, it may be.
But for my part I dislike glitter and gilt.'

'Spelling guilt with a *u* or without it?'
asked Pygmalion.

'We must ask Cosmo how to spell it,' said
the duke. 'He knows everything.'

The path had opened and formed a slop-
ing stretch of sward, in the midst of which,
on a little eminence, stood a group of noble
limes. Glimpses of the river peeped here
and there through the wood. The lime trees
threw a wide stretch of shade around them.
A hum of bees in the upper branches filled
the air with a slumbrous murmur. A delicious breeze, rich with sylvan scents, was
blowing across the stream. Cosmo's banquet,
spread beneath the trees, glistened—a mass
of rich colour—amid the soft surrounding
tints.

'You must all come to the top of the hill,'

said Cosmo, 'and get the view of the river
and the most picturesque little church you
ever saw.   It is a tiny affair, but as old as
the hills—as old, at any rate, as the Heptarchy.'

'The Heptarchy!' cried Miss Bond, awed
into momentary decorum by the idea of such
antiquity; 'and do you mean that none of
you people have ever made a pilgrimage to
it before?'

The scene was indeed romantic enough to
fire a less ready enthusiasm than Miss Bond's.
At the foot of the hill, but a few yards away,
closely neighboured by overhanging trees
and half buried in its own ivy, stood a little
country church.   A few half-obliterated grave-
stones and a couple of yews, whose wide-
spreading gnarled branches bespoke the
flight of centuries, gave the scene its complet-
ing touches of quiet, melancholy rest.   There
were but few signs of modern use; though a
rough road and one or two converging paths

from different quarters of the wood showed
how a congregation, or rather such modest
attempt at one as the narrow limits of the
building allowed, might assemble. Few evidently now frequented it. A village, so tra-
dition said, for which it had been built, had
disappeared before a Norman monarch's
sporting requirements in the way of undisturbed deer-coverts. Religious scruples had
saved the church; it served now, probably,
for an occasional service to some outlying
hamlet; but the deserted look and untrodden
paths showed that few were the worshippers
who sought this unpretentious shrine. Some
children stood in the porch, however, and it
was obvious that some use of it was being
made to-day.

'The Heptarchy!' exclaimed Miss Bond
reverentially, as she stood and gazed; 'I adore
old things of every sort, especially churches.
I must go down and indulge in some
romance.'

'We will all go afterwards,' said Cosmo,
'and be as romantic as you please. At
present the claims of the practical, in the
shape of lunch, are not to be denied. See,
there is Franz sending to tell us that it is
ready.'

This small diversion had given M. Franz
the necessary time to put the finishing touches
to several delicacies whose perfection would
have been endangered by an instant's delay.
Everything was now complete, and the party
soon disposed itself around a banquet which
even its critical author, as he stood compla-
cently watching its consumption from a distance, admitted to be worthy of his master,
the occasion, and himself.

The champagne began to flow. The
guests, with appetites quickened by the
fatigues of the morning, busied themselves
with courageous essays into the unimagined
refinements of M. Franz's *menu*. The good
cheer told its tale in a general rise of spirits.

The duke was happy, and made M. Franz
happy by demanding a second help of a new
pudding, expressly devised in his honour for
the occasion, and christened Egeria. The
stream of conversation ran quick, strong,
and boisterous. Mrs. Araby's venom became
profuse, Miss Bond's fun uproarious.

The attractions of the repast diverted
attention from the disagreeable fact that
the clouds were gathering thickly overhead.
The gloom now suddenly increased, and,
before luncheon was over, sundry ominous
growls and rumbles announced that the fair
promise of the morning was not to be fulfilled.
The storm, after all, was going to be to-day.
It grew darker and darker. Already a drop
had fallen on Mrs. Backhouse's dress.

'*Actum est!*' cried Florian; 'the most
beautiful toilette in Europe will be ruined!'

What was to be done? The launch had
not yet arrived; the carriages had been sent
off to a village, a mile away, till after lunch.

Nobody had paid a cloudless morning the bad compliment of bringing an umbrella.

'Fortunately,' cried Cosmo, 'we can, like other destitutes, take refuge in the church! We shall be an interesting addition to the congregation! Mrs. Araby, let us fly! None of you would forgive me if I betrayed you to a drenching, and I should never forgive myself.'

A vivid flash, which gave the disagreeable impression of lightning being ubiquitous, and a crashing peal of thunder close overhead, put an end to hesitation. The rain began to fall. There was a stampede for the church. The doors, happily, were open. Service was in course of performance. In another instant the whole party were safely established beneath a welcome roof. The building was small, shabby to the last degree, and tenanted only by scanty groups — a little row of children, a few old women and labourers. Olivia entered the first pew which offered,

and found herself alone in one of those high-
walled enclosures, which the exclusivism of
our grandfathers considered the fittest for
purposes of public prayer.   The building
must have been dark at all times, shut in on
every side by huge, over-towering trees, the
narrow windows curtailed still further by
encroaching ivy.   But from without, just now,
but little light was to be had.   It was dark,
and grew darker every moment.   The
humble ceremony progressed despite the
crash of thunder and the pelting rain outside.
The school children, clustered round the
altar, assisted in the modest rite.   The
silence, the safety, the solitude, struck upon
Olivia's senses with a sudden feeling of
exquisite relief.   The familiar words fell upon
her ear like voices from a vanished world.
A sense of peace, of rest, came over her.
For a while she was safe.   The rain, happily,
showed no symptom of abating.   The service
would last another half-hour at the least.   An

interval of quiet was assured—a respite,
however short-lived, from the disagreeable
surroundings of the rest of the day. Priest
and people knelt to pray; Olivia followed
their example. To pray? Was prayer,
then, still an employment for reasonable
beings? Was the side of things to which
prayer belonged, with which religion had to
do, still a reality? Is there still a world
where the unseen, the invisible, the intangible,
the aspirations of pious souls seeking for
good, struggling through imperfection and
failure towards its attainment, the patient
fortitude of the unhappy, the penitent's self-
searchings, the martyr's enthusiasm, are
actual living forces, not the mere fictions of
half-crazed brains, the joke of cynics, the
contempt of philosophers? Has man a soul
and a future, a duty to God, to his fellow-
man, to himself? Is conscience the voice of
God speaking within the soul, not a phrase
for the scruples of the timorous, the hesitation

of the cowardly? Is life an awful glimpse
of eternity, of vast eternities, stretching far
away behind and before, a moment's revelation of unknowable, impenetrable mysteries,
not the fortuitous concourse of a few atoms
into a fleeting phantom, for which 'I know
not and I care not' is the appropriate creed,
and 'Let us eat and drink, for to-morrow
we die' the only rational philosophy? Is
religion a reality, the only reality, amid the
phantasms of existence, or the last flicker of
expiring superstitions at which civilised mankind can only smile? And, if a reality, what
were the people among whom Olivia's lot was
now cast? What was he to whose care she
was about to commit herself, body and soul,
with whom she was to face the actualities
of the present, the possibilities of the future?
What were her present companions? Was
there anything which could awe them to a
seriousness, or melt them to a tender mood?
Was there anything at which they would

not sneer ?—anything but the material in which they believed ?—anything beyond the pleasures of sense for which they cared ?

The service went on, prayer and chant and hymn. How familiar those sounds, how dear ! They recalled the Sunday afternoons at her father's church. Those afternoons ! How far they seemed to have vanished into the limbo of the past ! Yet they, at least, were real. This had been the real part of Olivia's life. She had lived a phantasmal, an unreal existence ever since. Those times came back upon her now, so vivid, so living, that they crowded out the present : some summer evenings when she had walked with her father across the fields, and he had been in an especially charming mood. Those evenings had seemed delightful then, but now they gleamed with the very light of Paradise. He sat by her once again. He held her hand. He was lying on his sofa while she sang to him. He was reciting some well-loved passage. He was reading to her from some favourite book. She was singing the songs he loved to hear. Olivia bent her head ; the tears began to flow. What a life had this been, and what a companion ! How peaceful, solemn, pure ; how cheered by a noble philosophy, how stirred by noble aspirations and noble hopes ! Beside it, how like a horrid nightmare seemed the life of which she was now tasting, the people with whom she now consorted. These men— cynical, cold, incredulous of good, of generous motive, of loyal act, who sneered at virtue as a pretence, at religion as a dream of savages, who threw off every trammel of creed or custom. Were they the better, the nobler, for their so-called emancipation, for their enlightened selfishness, their scorn of all that mankind has held sacred, their scoffing contempt for all that which awes the mind, that checks the hand of passion, that inter- feres with animal pleasure ? These women

—Mrs. Araby, with her poisoned jokes, her
ruthless sarcasms, her tongue of evil, her eye
of malice; Miss Bond, with her coarse
effrontery; Isabella, with her mean contrivances and ignoble aims; the duke, with
his cynical selfishness; Cosmo, with wicked
glittering eyes. Olivia thought of Lady
Heriot—serene, gentle, refined, courageous,
but with how different a courage from the
senseless indifference of the mundane throng
around her. How calm, how resigned, how
hopeful, how truly great! 'Death stands
above me,' she had once said to Olivia in a
confidential moment—

"Death stands above me, whispering low
I know not what into my ear;
Of his strange language all I know
Is there is not a word of fear." '

How did her present companions look at
death but as one degrading incident of an
existence made up of degradations! What
would Lady Heriot have thought of these

people ?   What would she have thought of
Olivia's predicament ?

.   .   .

A sudden light shone in upon her and lit
up her soul with the radiance of hope.   It
had all the suddenness of an inspiration.
From whence did it come and how ?   Her
fate was not irretrievably fixed.   There was
still a door of escape ; salvation might be
achieved.   Of late the cup of life had been
full of distasteful ingredients.   She had never
known true happiness, contentment, peace of
soul, since her engagement.   She had entered
on it, had been hurried into it, betrayed into
it, rashly, ignorantly.   It was open to her
still to draw back, if fuller knowledge, riper
experience warned her from a disastrous self-
surrender.   She had discovered many things
about herself, many about her lover, since
that promise had been given.   They had
altered her view ; they had filled her with
fear, distrust, sometimes actual dislike.   She

might yet be free.   Her heart leapt up in
exultation at the thought.   'Leave this land
of false enchantment,' an inward monitor
seemed to cry ; 'turn your back on these
false joys, these dangerous companions, these
unreal pleasures.   Seek happiness elsewhere,
or forego the search.   You can do this, you
dare to do it, you must.   You will need
courage, strength, heroism.   Be courageous,
heroic.'   The thought spread over Olivia's
mind like some welcome stream flowing on
to the parched soil, carrying with it refreshment, renovation, life.   Hope, joy, radiance
ineffable broke in upon her soul.   Deliverance
was still achievable.   Her fate was still in her
own hands.

Olivia went out of church inspired with a
new idea.   Ruin—if indeed ruin was now
before her—was still to be escaped.   She
resolved, cost what it might, to escape it.
She was a hopeful, happy woman, with a
brave resolve.

The storm was over. Some carriages
had arrived to convey the party to the launch,
where welcome tea was awaiting them. They
became very merry as they steamed down the
river to Cosmo's villa. The *contretemps* of
the afternoon had, to some extent, marred
the perfection of the day's arrangements, but
it reacted on the gentlemen's spirits. Nothing
is so provocative of mirth as a small misfortune, well got through—a crisis that proves
not too critical for good humour to surmount.
The ladies' dresses were saved, so that the
misfortune had been a very small one.
Cosmo's luncheon had served its purpose
before the downpour reduced the *débris* to
undistinguishable ruins. M. Franz alone,
who got his feet wet and caught a violent
cold, breathed a deeper vow than ever of
detestation of the English climate, and contempt for the English habit of feeding, like
animals, in the open air. The English guests
appeared, however, if one might judge from

their hilarity, to consider that all things had
gone as they ought.   Florian threw off the
poet and asked several conundrums which
had never been heard before, and which
served to amuse London drawing-rooms for
the next fortnight.   M. Duc delivered his
famous monologue—'l'homme qui pleure'—
with inimitable verve.   Dodo produced his
banjo and sang a comic song, which Thérèsa
had rendered celebrated at the Palais-Royal,
and which that enterprising young gentleman had gone to Paris on purpose to learn
direct from its illustrious performer.   It was
his *chef-d'œuvre—Pst-Pst—m'amie* ; it was
lively ; it was rollicking ; it was audacious ;
it went far, a little too far, perhaps, to be
quite in good form ; but this was not an
occasion to be particular, and anything was
better than not being amused.   There was a
roar of applause as the performance closed.

'My blushes,' said Mrs. Araby, 'like the
moonlight, are hidden by the clouds, but I

beg everybody to understand that I am blushing. Dodo, I blush for you.'

'And so do I,' said Mrs. Backhouse; 'I hope he is blushing for himself.'

'I am sorry,' said the duke, 'that I cannot pay you the compliment of blushing, even in the dark. I have forgotten how that juvenile tribute to propriety is paid. Dodo's performance had but a single fault, and a good one —it was too short.'

'It was broader than it was long,' said Florian—'the fashionable shape for comic songs. I vote that we encore it.'

Olivia, little disturbed by the surrounding hilarity, sat peacefully in the gloom, busied with her own thoughts, and enjoying an inward cheerfulness that was all her own.

CHAPTER XXXVI

MISS BOND IS CONFIDENTIAL

'When the Devil of my youth
Had set me on those mountain peaks of hope,
All glittering with the dawn dew, all erect
And famished for the moon.'

SILENCE reigned in Cosmo's villa. The ladies
had vanished to their rooms for the duties of
the toilette and the pleasures of repose. Isabella Heriot, for once, was sufficiently tired
to be glad of an interval of quiet, and to
remember, at her ease, that even an informal
occasion demands a well-considered *déshabille*.
Mrs. Backhouse was intending to crown the
triumphs of the day with a tea-gown, the
lovely freshness and flowing outlines of which
had not as yet been revealed to mortal eye.

Several of the other ladies would do their
best not to be eclipsed by Mrs. Backhouse.
Olivia, inspired by no such ambition, was
ready to descend long before her cousin had
accomplished her preparation for this interesting contest. She was longing to escape.
Her room felt oppressive, suffocating. Outside a river breeze was stirring the tree-tops
with a delicious murmur. The storm of the
afternoon had given place to an exquisite
evening. The moon was floating through a
fleecy sky. The last clouds were sinking in
the horizon. The terrace, the marble steps,
the lawns, the river beyond, were bathed in
soft floods of light. The garden promised an
undisturbed retreat, a solitary half-hour for
the rest of weary spirits, the restoration of
shattered nerves. Olivia threw a shawl
around her and prepared to fly. The hope
of solitude, however, was illusory. As Olivia
crossed the hall to the wide windows that
opened upon the terrace Miss Bond emerged

from the drawing-room.   She evidently wished
to be confidential.

'We are the first,' she said ; 'not a soul is
to be found.   I was making for the garden.
We can sit and talk in the colonnade.   Let
me come with you.'

'I have something to say to you,' continued Miss Bond as soon as they had found
a seat.   'You have not enjoyed to-day.   I
saw it all.   It was not likely that you should.
You have disliked us all, and we have
deserved disliking.   For my part, I am
furious with Mrs. Araby for her behaviour.
A joke is a joke, but her jokes are past
bearing.   She has a grudge against Mr. de
Renzi—an old grudge.   They are sworn
foes.   But that is no excuse for being
brutal, as I consider that she was this
morning.'

'I thought her rather rude,' said Olivia ;
'but brutal ?'

'She was brutal to all of you,' said Miss

Bond—' you, Mr. de Renzi, and poor Theresa
Backhouse.'

'Mrs. Backhouse!' cried Olivia. 'What
had she to do with it?'

'Do you not know?' said her companion.
'You surely must.'

'No,' said Olivia, 'I know nothing. What
is it? Do tell me.'

'Do you really mean that you do not
know that Mrs. Backhouse is dreadfully
aggrieved at Mr. de Renzi deserting her?
Poor creature, she is inconsolable!'

'Deserting her!' cried Olivia. 'What
can you mean? Why, she is a married
woman!'

'Which makes the desertion all the more
poignant. Married women like desertion as
little as the rest of us. And Mrs. Backhouse's desertion was a bad one. Mr. de
Renzi was devoted to her last season. They
were mutually devoted, a real serious, *boná-
fide* devotion. It lasted till you appeared

upon the scene.   Then he threw her over, and
was on with the new love before he was off
with the old.   It is an old trick of his.   Mrs.
Backhouse, who is sentimental, and vain into
the bargain, naturally did not like it.   She
poses as a martyr, and she is foolish enough
to proclaim her misfortunes to all her intimate
friends, who naturally think it far too good a
joke to keep to themselves.   But that is no
reason why Mrs. Araby should chaff them
both in public, especially with you there to
hear it!   Yes, it was brutal!'

Olivia sat shuddering in silence.

'After all,' continued her companion,
alarmed at getting no response, 'it was
nothing remarkable.   Anyhow, it is no concern of yours, or of anybody's, except as
a good joke.   All the men do it.   Poor
Theresa Backhouse is not the first, nor will
she be the last!   As for Mr. de Renzi, he
is such an old offender that everybody is
delighted to see him caught at last.   It was

a triumph to catch him, a real triumph! I envy you!'

Olivia sprang to her feet with the gesture of one who shrinks from a revelation of horror.

'Now,' she cried, 'I see the point of Mrs. Araby's joke! Thank you for telling me. I agree with you. It was brutal!'

'I fear that I have shocked you,' said Miss Bond, in surprise at the vehement seriousness of Olivia's tone. 'You must not take things of that sort seriously.'

'No?' said Olivia. 'What, then, are the things which one ought to be serious about when one is going to be married? Is there anything?'

'Not, at any rate, the flirtations of your husband—past, present, or to come. That is the first law of modern married life. Society has decreed it. But do you mean that you knew nothing—nothing?'

'Nothing!' said Olivia. 'How should I? Those who should enlighten me conspire to keep me in the dark. What is there to know ?'

'Forbid it, Innocence!' cried Miss Bond, 'that I should tell. I have told you too much already. Forget it. Ignorance is bliss; such bliss be yours. Here, by the way, is your happy lover approaching, who will owe me an eternal grudge if I rob him of a *tête-à-tête*. I will yield him my place before he discovers me.'

Miss Bond retreated to the house. De Renzi came and took her place. He was in his gayest mood. 'Olivia mia!' he cried, 'and by yourself—

"a lady of the lake,
Sole sitting by the shores of old romance "—

waiting for me to come and be romantic in the moonlight. Tell me now, have you enjoyed it all, despite the rain ?'

'Pretty well,' said Olivia; then suddenly turning to him, 'No, Claude, I will tell you the truth. I must do so. I have *not* enjoyed it. I have been wretched. I am in the depths of low spirits.'

De Renzi with difficulty repressed an outbreak of provocation at this unexpected announcement. 'Your spirits are capricious, Olivia. I hoped that you would be pleased. Everybody else has been delighted. You have had everything that human wit can contrive for your enjoyment. What could you wish more? What has been the matter?'

'You must forgive me,' said Olivia. 'I have been ill at ease. Good spirits will not come at command, not at *my* command at any rate.'

'Come now, you dear piece of perversity, admit the truth. You had resolved not to enjoy it, had you not?'

'No,' said Olivia; 'believe me. I was bound to try. I did try. But there are some things which are fatal to good spirits.'

'For instance?' asked De Renzi.

'A doubt, a suspicion in the heart of a woman who loves. If only you could clear them away from mine!'

'How can I,' cried her lover, 'when I have no notion of the cause? However, be the cause, the fancied cause, what it may, your doubts are baseless, the phantasm of imagination, the forgeries of jealousy!'

'Well, then,' said Olivia, 'I believe that I am jealous!'

'Jealous!' cried De Renzi; 'you jealous, and to me!'

'Yes,' said Olivia, 'that is one of the things that disquiet me. I am jealous.'

'Impossible!' cried De Renzi. 'It is a barbarous passion, fit only for a blackamoor like Othello, and as obsolete as the mega-therium. Forswear it, Olivia, I implore you. We shall never have a moment's peace. I am never jealous! I surrendered you to the duke, to Cosmo, this afternoon, without a pang. And jealousy to me—what a conception! Don't you know that I am fanatically in love with you, and care not a straw for all the other women in the world? What makes you doubt me? What can I do to still your doubts?'

Olivia was in no mood for banter. 'Do you know,' she said, 'that in all our intercourse you have never told me yet one single word about your past?'

'My past!' cried De Renzi, with a mock-heroic air. 'Horrid subject! It is dead, gone, forgotten; leave it to the dust, the ivy, and the bats. I have buried it. Spare me a resurrection!'

'The women you have loved before you loved me—is there no one that I have a right to be jealous of?'

'The women that I have loved!' cried De Renzi with a laugh. 'Olivia, you touch a tender point; you press too far. Suffice it that you are despot, supreme and unquestioned, of a heart that owns no mistress but yourself. What need you, what would you have more ?'

'I have just heard something,' said Olivia, whose seriousness of manner increased as De Renzi took refuge in levity, 'something which gives a solid form to doubts and suspicions that have been floating in my mind—in my heart. They have been gathering strength; they have been very strong to-day. I ought to tell it to you. It may be false.'

'It *is* false,' cried De Renzi with vehemence, 'if it is anything that impugns my devotion to you. Tell it me and let me reassure your confidence, since it needs reassurance.'

'You remember Mrs. Araby's attack on you this morning?'

'Yes,' said De Renzi, with some uneasiness in his tone; 'she is an old witch with the tongue of the devil. She ought to be drowned on a broomstick.'

'I have been told what she meant—that there is one whom, a few months ago, you were supposed to love, whom you led to love you, whom even now you regard with affection, who regards your marriage as a cruel desertion of herself, and me as the robber of her rights. Tell me if it is so, that I may release you from your engagement.'

'This is too much!' cried De Renzi in a passion. 'You carry your rights too far. I will not be questioned by any one, Olivia, not even by you. There are things on which no man will—no man of honour ought to—submit to be catechised. I decline to say a word as to my past relations to any one, except that I was speaking the truth, as a loyal gentleman, when I offered you my love and asked for yours. There are some friendships which even marriage does not obliterate.'

'And the desertion?' asked Olivia. 'May I disbelieve that part of the story?'

'You must believe or disbelieve what you please,' said De Renzi. 'I decline to be questioned.'

'It is, surely, no unreasonable question,' said Olivia, 'standing as we do to each other.'

'That is as people think,' said De Renzi. 'Anyhow, I will not answer it.'

'That is answer enough,' said Olivia. Her voice had the solemnity of a death-sentence.

A gong sounded. Cosmo was standing at the window, and called them. De Renzi started to his feet. It was a welcome staving-off of a crisis, for which neither party was prepared. Both felt that it was a relief that their dispute should be peremptorily brought to a close.

'We must go,' De Renzi said. 'I will come to you the first thing to-morrow. You will feel differently then, I hope.'

Cosmo was awaiting them at the window. 'Forgive me,' he said, 'for interrupting you. Will you take Miss Hillyard in to dinner?'

CHAPTER XXXVII

THE STORM BURSTS

'Ah ! what a vulgar thing does courage seem, when we see
nations buying and selling it at a shilling a day.   Ah !
what a sublime thing does courage seem, when some
fearful summons on the great deeps of life carries a
man, as if running before a hurricane, up to the giddy
crest of some tumultuous crisis, from which lie two
courses, and a voice says to him audibly, " One way lies
hope ; take the other, and mourn for ever ! "   How
grand a triumph if, even then, amid the raving of all
around him and the frenzy of the danger, the man is
able to confront his situation, is able to retire for a
moment into solitude with God, and to seek his counsel
from Him.'

THE worst and longest day has its end.
Olivia saw the end of hers.   The party
had dispersed.   The gentlemen had gone
away to London, De Renzi amongst the rest.
The lovely tea-gowns vanished with their
owners.   Peace reigned in the luxurious

corridors of Cosmo's little palace — peace,
and kindly sleep with its sweet anodyne for
human woes.   In one room of the villa, however, there was no thought of sleep, but the
intense activity of throbbing pulses, overwrought nerves, excited brains.   Mrs. Heriot
had been all day on thorns about Olivia,
first disappointed, next angry, finally alarmed.
Olivia had belied the brilliant hopes that had
been entertained on her behalf.   She had
tried in vain to hide her gloomy mood.   She
had not been brilliant, she had not been
amusing, she had not been even cheerful.
The gentlemen who tried to get on terms
with her had retired in discomfiture.   The
duke, in the course of the morning, had
invited her for a stroll, but soon brought
her back, and made no further effort at
politeness.   Mr. Cosmo could make nothing
of her.   Her rising reputation had sunk to
zero.   Claude de Renzi must, Mrs. Heriot
felt, be annoyed at his future wife playing so

inglorious a part, so completely belying his expectations of what she might and would achieve. Such a lapse was inexcusable. Mrs. Araby's jokes at De Renzi had not, certainly, been in the best of taste; but girls must learn to take a joke, and even a neophyte in the mysteries of polite society might be expected to make allowance for Mrs. Araby. She was a chartered libertine in the matter of conversation. Her witticisms were too racy not to be condoned. Anyhow, resent it or not, as Olivia might think fit, she was bound, in the circumstances, to keep her resentment to herself. But she had shown temper, and shown it in the one way that was unforgivable, by being dull, by being a non-conductor to social electricity. The anxieties of a chaperon are — Mrs. Heriot ruefully acknowledged to herself, as she tapped at the door of Olivia's room—a great deal more serious than people who have not the management of refractory

young beauties are accustomed to believe.
Just now Olivia was in a refractory mood,
and Mrs. Heriot was too anxious to sleep
in peace without ascertaining explicitly to
what extent her refractoriness had gone and
was about to go.

Her worst anticipations were justified by
Olivia's appearance. She was sitting, appar-
ently, just where she had sat down when, half
an hour before, she had entered the room.
Her hair, which always seized the first opportunity of rebellion, was dishevelled ; her eyes
bore the mark of tears ; her cheeks were
pale ; her appearance bespoke distress, agitation, the restlessness of perplexity, the courage
of despair. Mrs. Heriot thought it well to
veil the purpose of her visit by an air of
indifference. She put down her candle and
began at once to chatter as if she had merely
come for a gossip.

'Are you dreadfully tired, Olivia ? For
my part, I am dead beat. The morning was

so sultry, and thunder always upsets me ; and what thunder! It rings in my head still. I shall not be able to sleep for hours, I am certain. But what a Providence that church was! We saved our dresses, which is something ; but, to tell the truth, I was terrified. I am an arrant coward about lightning when one is out of doors. That last flash actually blinded me. However, the whole thing was delightful, was it not? Cosmo is really perfect in his own house. You have got over your dislike to him by this time. But, Olivia, what is the matter with you? You sit there as white as a ghost; why don't you speak? Are you feeling faint?'

'No,' said Olivia, 'it is nothing ; but I am as tired as you are. The day has been too long. I am over-tired. I did not find the picnic as delightful as you did.'

'No?' said Mrs. Heriot. 'I was afraid you were not enjoying yourself. But they were all kind to you, were they not?'

'Kind!' cried Olivia. 'What kindness! I thought them detestable.'

'Come, come,' said her companion, 'is not that too sweeping? The American girl's slang is vulgar, of course, but that is the fun of it: and Mrs. Araby's jokes and stories! You must not think about them. She is an old offender, and a privileged one. She does it to every one; and no one minds. She has done it from time immemorial. I don't defend her. If it was any one but Mrs. Araby, people would call her a vulgar old wretch.'

'She *is* a vulgar old wretch,' cried Olivia with vehemence, 'and a cruel one. She tried to wound me, to insult me; she meant it; I could feel it. They are a hateful set, Isabella —bad, coarse, heartless. I have passed a miserable day, and am thoroughly wretched.'

'You are thoroughly tired,' said her companion, seriously apprehensive of a coming explosion, 'and so am I—too tired to discuss Mrs. Araby. All the same, she was not meaning to be rude to you. She was only chaffing Claude—surely there was no harm in that.'

'No harm!' cried Olivia.

'No harm,' said Mrs. Heriot with a laugh, taking up her candle and preparing to depart. 'A little chaff hurts no one; Claude as little as any. He deserves it. Good-night!'

'Stop!' cried Olivia; 'I have something to say to you. I had better say it at once. I will tell you what the harm is.'

'Well,' said Mrs. Heriot, coming back and shutting the door, conscious that the much-dreaded crisis had arrived, 'what is it?'

'I have heard something to-day,' said Olivia, 'which entitles me to ask you a question. What is the story of Claude de Renzi and Mrs. Backhouse? What did Mrs. Araby mean this morning when she raised a laugh at his expense and mine, and Mrs. Backhouse's?'

'What?' said Mrs. Heriot. 'She meant, I suppose, that Claude de Renzi is about to unite himself to a most impetuous young lady. I wish him joy of you if you intend to behave as you are doing now.'

'You evade my question,' said Olivia. 'What has there been between them? There *is* something. You have concealed it from me, Isabella. You have not told me the truth. I learnt it to-day by accident. Am I to marry without knowing what it is? Am I to take him blindfold, not knowing whether he is mine; and if mine, when he became so, whether his heart is his own to give me? I have been feeling, for weeks past, that there was something wrong. I felt it most of all to-day. Claude de Renzi is not what I believed, nor am I what he thought. I shall never make him a good wife. Suppose that I were to break off my engagement, Isabella, may I look to you to help me?'

Mrs. Heriot felt the crisis to be indeed

acute. She came and sat down on the sofa
by Olivia. For some moments she could not
say a word. Surprise, disappointment, anger,
alarm, were too much for her. Olivia sat
looking at. her, intrepid, excited, insistent.
At last she spoke. 'Break off your engagement? Olivia, you have taken leave of
your senses; you must be wandering; you
do not know what you are saying! It is
impossible that you can be in earnest!'

'Earnest!' cried Olivia; 'never more
bitterly in earnest. It is a question of life
or death for me. But would you help me?'

'Help you!' said Mrs. Heriot. 'You may
rely upon it that neither I nor Valentine will
ever let you do anything so mad. We will
never allow it.'

'I feared that it would be so,' said Olivia.
'Have mercy on me, Isabella; I am alone in
the world; I am in dire need of help; I must
act for myself; it concerns myself alone.'

'Yourself alone!' cried Mrs. Heriot, whose

anger-storm was rapidly gathering to the
bursting-point of indignation. ' Do·you know
what you are saying? what it is that you
talk so glibly about doing? Do you know
that it means your ruin, your loss of the best
chance a girl in your position ever had—so
good that I am constantly lost in astonish-
ment at your good luck? It means disgracing yourself, disgracing us—insulting Claude
de Renzi in the face of the world—alienating
him—alienating his family—figuring before
society as a mad woman! It is impossible,
however. You are not yourself; you are
overwrought. Go to bed now and to sleep,
and wake up, please, in your right mind : but
remember that, if by to-morrow morning this
piece of lunacy has not quitted you, you will
have to go to some other house than mine to
commit this frantic act—to offer this gross
affront to the man who has loaded you with
kindness.'

' But my question,' said Olivia. ' Do you

mean that there has been—that there is
nothing between Claude de Renzi and Mrs.
Backhouse that ought to make me hesitate
if I knew it?'

Mrs. Heriot, in spite of her efforts to
preserve an unaltered aspect, coloured up.
'I do mean it,' she said vehemently. 'Are
you going to listen to every piece of silly
gossip that venomous tongues, like Mrs.
Araby's, set agoing. Theresa Backhouse is
an idiot, the worst sort of idiot, a sentimental
one. If she chooses to imagine herself in
love with De Renzi, what has that to do with
you or with him? Plenty of women, I daresay, have been in the same predicament. If
she was not a fool she would not care to dis-
grace herself by such an exhibition. She
likes to pose as broken-hearted. She has
not sense to see that she is making herself
ridiculous. Do you remember that she is a
married woman?'

'Only too well,' said Olivia; 'but is it true,

Isabella, that only a few months ago Claude
de Renzi was in love with her?'

Mrs. Heriot's passion at last blazed out.
'How, in the name of common sense,' she
cried, 'can I tell, or any one? And if he
was, do you expect your husband to have
been an innocent all his life, a nursery
innocent? to have looked at no woman till
you appeared upon the scene? to offer you a
virgin heart? Believe me, such men exist
nowhere but in goody story-books, nor such
women either. They would not be worth
twopence if they did. How long is it, Olivia,
since you were, or believed yourself, in love
with Jack? Think of that and be rational.
At any rate, be warned!'

Mrs. Heriot turned and left the room
without another word. Olivia, again alone—
her cousin's menace ringing angrily in her
ear—set herself to review the position and to
rally her resources of fortitude for this crisis
of her fate.

CHAPTER XXXVIII

A LOVER'S DOUBT

'Let me not to the marriage of true minds
Admit impediments: Love is not love,
Which alters when it alteration finds,
Or bends with the remover to remove.'

DE RENZI travelled home that Sunday night revolving many things. He had been aggrieved by the scene with Olivia—aggrieved and alarmed. She had revealed a new phase of character. De Renzi had no wish for a wife with a grievance—for a wife who would insist too rigidly on what she considered her rights, who would construe those rights exactingly, who would be unhappy if she considered that she did not get her due. The one thing which he did not intend to

do in marriage was to put an inconvenient
fetter on his personal liberty. He had no
idea of domesticating a recording angel.
He intended, by marrying Olivia, to in-
crease his enjoyments, not to surrender
his freedom.

Olivia's scruples, demands, doubts, might
prove an awkward obstruction in the pleasant
journey of existence. He admired, he loved
her; but neither love nor admiration would
carry him the length of submission to a
domestic tyrant. He was making a romantically disinterested marriage. But how if the
romance assumed an unexpected phase of
severity, of strictness, of immoderate demands,
of inconvenient scruples? Was it certain
that Claude was not doing what of all things
he, no less than his father, detested—making
a bad bargain?

De Renzi could not think of his late interview with Olivia without resentment. She
had been unreasonable; her demands were

outrageous. To comply with them would be
a fatal surrender of all lawful liberties. Olivia
was courageous ; but then, if one was to
marry a courageous woman, it would never
do to begin by giving in to her whims, by
submitting to defeat. Her husband must
be courageous too. Olivia's demands about
Mrs. Backhouse were a whim, a jealous
whim. He would not gratify it, nor in truth
could he. He was feeling tender, remorseful
about Mrs. Backhouse. He was seriously
sorry to have given her pain. Their last
interview had been a painful one. Mrs.
Backhouse had never looked more lovely ;
her beautiful azure eyes had filled with tears,
and her voice had trembled with ill-sup-
pressed emotion. De Renzi had no touch
of the cynical brutality which could sneer at
such emotion, or point a rough moral as to
the rightful retribution which befalls a married
woman who chooses to be idyllic. He had,
he was forced to admit to himself, behaved

badly to Mrs. Backhouse—badly according
to his own standard of what was right, fair,
permissible.   He had shown her marked
attentions the year before.   Their mutual
liking had been a recognised fact.   Their
intimacy—temporarily cut short by Olivia's
appearance at the Pines—had speedily re-
vived.   It had ripened into a flirtation—
unluckily, on Mrs. Backhouse's part, into
something more.   It was foolish and weak
of her, no doubt ; but this scarcely made it
pleasant for De Renzi.   For a time he had
been really devoted to her, and had surrendered himself to the agreeable pastime of
playing at love—of petting a woman whom
nature intended to be petted.   Now he had
deserted her.   She could never, of course,
have supposed that their intimacy was to
interfere with his marriage when the time
arrived.   But the time had arrived with unexpected promptitude.   Their intimacy had
closed with a cruel abruptness.   Claude

thought of it with regret and discomfort.
Mrs. Backhouse chose to consider herself
heart-broken, and, what was worse, to show
the broken fragments of her heart to sundry
friendly eyes. Nevertheless Claude would
stand by her. Nothing should force him to
belittle a woman to whom he had paid attention, to ignore his past feelings for her. If,
despite of them, he was prepared to marry
her, Olivia ought to appreciate the value
of the compliment. She could, in reason,
demand no further sacrifice. On the other
hand, if she proved exacting, unreasonable,
and prepared, in case she could not get her
own way, to break off the engagement, De
Renzi determined that it would not be wise
to oppose her resolution.

So ran De Renzi's thoughts as he journeyed
Londonwards. On reaching home he went
straight to his desk, took out Olivia's portrait,
sat gazing at it for some instants, and straight-
way repented, in mental sackcloth and ashes,

of his resentful mood.   Give her up, indeed!
Wayward, uncertain, exacting, oppressive—
what you will—he loved her, and love
welcomes every expedient rather than surrender.

CHAPTER XXXIX

FAREWELL

'Silvia is too fair, too true, too holy
To be corrupted by my worthless gifts ;
When I protest true loyalty to her,
She twits me with my falsehood to my friend ;
When to her beauty I commend my vows,
She bids me think how I have been forsworn
In breaking faith with Julia whom I loved.'

OLIVIA had spent a sleepless night in becoming more and more frightened. Had Claude met her responsively and sympathetically, the night before, she might still have been reassured, brought back to her allegiance, to hope and happiness, if not to absolute confidence. But the interview had done nothing but intensify her alarm, strengthen her conviction that she was going wrong, and that safety lay only in retreat. Her conversation

with Mrs. Heriot had not tended to soothe
her nerves or allay her apprehensions. No
word on the subject passed as the two
travelled up to town next day.

De Renzi came at the appointed time.
His angry mood of the previous night had
melted away. He was wishing only for
reconciliation. The lover was once more in
the ascendant. He had convinced himself
that Olivia's jealous mood was excusable, the
natural outbreak of lovable waywardness. It
could be appeased ; poor Theresa Backhouse's fancied wrongs could never be a
serious ground of alienation to people who
were as much in love as Olivia and
himself.

De Renzi, as Olivia came into the room,
looking miserable and frightened, yet beautiful, and bearing herself with dignity, felt
more than ever that to surrender her would
be impossible.

Still, things would not go smoothly.

Olivia was in a more difficult, a more un-compromising mood than on the previous day. She had been making up her mind. She saw clearly what she ought to do; she was nerved to do it. De Renzi felt speedily that the position was serious—defeat a not remote contingency.

'You must forgive me,' she said. 'You have done me many kindnesses. This will be the greatest of all. I have been to blame. Everybody else will blame me, I know. But you must understand and forgive. I told you that I had doubts. I put them aside. I hoped that they would vanish. I tried to believe that they had vanished. I was mistaken. They have still haunted me. Of late they have been stronger than ever. I have tried to silence them.'

'And in vain?' said De Renzi.

'In vain,' said Olivia; 'I feel greater doubts now than ever. I ought to tell you, ought I not?'

'Of course,' said De Renzi. 'What is the use of our going on with unexplained doubts between us? Are they doubts about me, or doubts about yourself? Yesterday your doubts were about me. I hope that I convinced you that they were groundless.'

'Doubts about us both,' said Olivia; 'gravest about myself. I distrust myself. I have told you so often. I have moods for which I cannot account—unknown currents that sway me. Of late I have been very un-happy—more unhappy, more anxious, more frightened than ever before in my life. I have been asking myself the cause.'

'And the answer?' said De Renzi.

'The answer, I believe, is that I am going wrong; we both are wrong. You are mistaken in me. I can never, I shall never be all you expect—all you see in me now, or did see in me a little while ago.'

'All I see now!' cried Claude. 'You are as charming to me as you ever were—as fascinating. But I am changed for you. I am not what you thought.'

'I was too dazzled to think,' said Olivia, 'to see, to judge. You were so good to me —so kind; your praise was so sweet, your will so strong. My will bent before it. I took for granted that you must be right; but I ought to have known.'

'To have known what?'

'To have known that it was impossible for our lives to be in harmony. Our tastes, our beliefs, our standards, are worlds apart. I in my inexperience—you with your full knowledge of every side, except of the sort of life that I have lived—the only one I can live happily. You forgive me for speaking so?'

'Forgive!' said De Renzi; 'I am begging you to speak. For my part, I do not know what these hopeless differences between us are. I know less of life than I supposed. What side of life is it which is so dear to you and a sealed book to me? Must it always remain a sealed book?'

'I was bred in a country home,' answered Olivia, 'and to village life. My father was a clergyman. We lived in retirement, he and I. I was always amongst the poor; we were very poor ourselves. Religion was our business, our inspiring thought, our consolation in many troubles, our hope. Many things are sacred to me which have no meaning to others; no meaning, I think, to you. Many things are dear, very dear to me, which are less than nothing to you. I have some fears, dreadful fears, which have no terrors for you. They have returned upon me with a vehemence which is like an inspiration. I dare not resist them. I should always be miserable if my life ignored them—if I allowed myself, as I have done too much of late, to live forgetting them. Yesterday brought it home to me. You meant it to be a day of happiness to me, of amusement, pleasure, success. It was a day of misery. I was wretched. The only happy moments I passed were those when I was kneeling in the little church, when we took refuge from the storm. I then learnt the cause of my unhappiness, and knew that I ought to ask you to release me. I beg you to do so.'

'It is no question of releasing,' said De Renzi; 'I am not fool enough to rest any claim on your promise if your heart belies it. But think before you take a step which must turn the current of both our lives—which would be a cruel blow to me. Last night you mentioned another motive, a motive of jealousy. Are you sure that it is not that which is prompting you?'

'That,' said Olivia, 'is one of our differences; it is a fatal one. I am jealous, I admit. You think it absurd. But I could never alter as to that. I could never accept your view. You think it nothing that another woman is aggrieved at my happiness—a

woman who was but so lately your friend,
who loves you now, whom you perhaps still
love. I should feel it sacrilege to accept
happiness so offered. A curse would be on
it and on me. I dare not. Will you release
me?'

'Release you,' cried De Renzi, 'and on
such a monstrous ground as that! Never,
never! Why spoil both our lives for a
fantastic whim of jealousy? for it is fantastic,
Olivia—fantastic and baseless. I love and
admire you as devoutly as ever woman was
loved. You know that I am in love with
you, fervently in love. You must know it.
I offer you everything I have or shall ever
have or be in life—I can do no more. What
does it signify what I have been in former
times before I loved you? What matter
past friendships, past intimacies, past affections, supposing them to have existed? You
have effaced them all. I swear to you that
they exist no more. I am yours and yours

alone. Why criticise my past? condone it;
forget it, as I have forgotten it. If you
love me as I do you——'

Olivia put up her hand with a deprecatory
gesture, and De Renzi's outburst came suddenly to a standstill.

'What is it?' he asked.

'That "if,"' said Olivia; 'everything
turns on that. I have been asking myself:
such love as yours demands a careful search
and an honest answer.'

'And the honest answer,' said De Renzi,
turning pale, for he knew that he was close
upon the crisis of his fate; 'tell me the
truth.'

'I will tell you the truth,' said Olivia,
'I owe it to you; it is the only reparation I
can make. It is a humiliating confession.'

'Confession, indeed! I absolve you be-
forehand.'

'You can never do that,' said Olivia; 'my
offence is unforgivable. When you speak of

loving me as you have just spoken, I feel
what a culprit I am ; how guilty I have been.
I have suffered, encouraged your love when
. . . I cannot return it.'

' I was a fool to say it!' cried De Renzi.
' Of course you do not feel for me as I do for
you. How should you ? It is not in nature
that you should ; but you must let me love
you, worship you. You will be mine at last.
Meanwhile I am content.'

' No,' said Olivia, ' believe me, it can
never be. I have searched into my heart.
I am confident now of what I suspected all
along. I wished to love you ; I wished to
be your wife, to share your honour, your
success, your triumphs. I admired you so
much. I was delighted, dazzled, over-
powered ; I have felt many things towards
you—gratitude, interest, admiration—but not
love.'

De Renzi stood silent and motionless, his
bloodless cheek alone betraying the intense

excitement which he was struggling to conceal.

'Not love?' he said at last; 'and is it impossible that love should ever come? What is there in our past friendship that tells you that it is impossible?'

'You keep me on the rack,' said Olivia. 'Have mercy; forgive me, I entreat you, and set me free.'

'You are free,' said De Renzi; 'I will torture you no more. Bad as you deem me, I am not bad enough to take advantage of a woman's promise, nor fool enough to accept a wife who comes to me full of doubts, scruples, and reluctance. Feeling as you do, you are perfectly right to break with me. It is well to do it before marriage instead of after.'

'Can you forgive me?' said Olivia.

'There is nothing to forgive,' said De Renzi. 'You have told me the truth; it is bitter, but I thank you for telling it. I shall

think of you always as I have from the first
moment I saw you—as I do now—as the
most perfect woman I have ever known.
Olivia, good-bye.'

Olivia's eyes were swimming with tears ;
her hand lingered in De Renzi's.

'Good-bye,' she said in broken tones.
'You have been very good to me ; you are
very good to me now. You have my
warmest gratitude.'

'Gratitude,' said De Renzi, 'is but the
ghost of love. We do well to part. Farewell.'

CHAPTER XL

‘ But, an’ you will not wed, I’ll pardon you—
Graze where you will, you shall not house with me.
Look to’t, think on’t, I do not use to jest.’

MRS. HERIOT began to feel that the fates
were against her. Her husband, when she
confided to him the awful intelligence of
Olivia’s recusancy, had displayed an unexpected independence, a view of the matter
which was wholly unsympathetic, antagonistic
to his wife’s. It was another instance, Mrs.
Heriot felt, of the way in which Valentine
always failed her at a pinch. She could
never screw his courage to the sticking place,
or silence his inconvenient scruples. He now

declared that Olivia must be left to do exactly what she pleased, and was in no case to be bullied.

'Bullied!' said Mrs. Heriot with some contempt in her tone. 'Who wants to bully her? but warned, I presume, that she is making a fool of herself.'

'How do we know that she is making a fool of herself?' said Valentine. 'She is the only person to judge of that. It is her affair, not ours. Remember, Isabella, I will not have her bullied.'

Mrs. Heriot made no reply. It was no good to argue with such a mood. For herself, if bullying could have prevented Olivia from throwing away a splendid prize, in mere caprice, Mrs. Heriot would have applied the most drastic form of it within her reach. She despised her husband; she sometimes felt inclined to hate him; she hated him now. Once more he was falling short of what might be expected of a reasonable being;

and unreasonableness, especially in a person whom one is obliged to obey, is always hateful.

It was expedient, however, Mrs. Heriot felt, to approach Olivia with other methods than the off-hand brutality of the previous night. The only chance lay in being conciliatory; and Mrs. Heriot, who had been watching nervously for De Renzi's departure, came, a few minutes later, into the drawing-room with gentle tones and looks, bent evidently on a policy of conciliation.

Olivia was sitting where De Renzi had left her, looking the picture of despair.

'Well, Olivia,' Mrs. Heriot said, 'have you two young people made up your quarrel satisfactorily? Why, I should like to know, are lovers such a quarrelsome race?'

'It is no case of quarrel,' said Olivia disconsolately; 'it is all at an end, Isabella. Mr. de Renzi has been most kind to me about it, but he quite agrees with me that, feeling as I do, it is impossible for me to go on.   It would be certain unhappiness for us both.'

'And you parted as friends?' asked Mrs. Heriot, fairly staggered by the explicitness of the announcement, and clinging to every remnant of hope in an almost desperate case.

'As good friends,' said Olivia.   'Mr. de Renzi thanked me for acting as I did.'

'He thanked you!' said Mrs. Heriot. 'Then reconciliation must be possible, surely?'

'We have nothing to reconcile,' said Olivia; 'we are agreed.   I told him all my feelings about it.'

'What feelings?' cried Mrs. Heriot, with whom the warnings of prudence and her husband's injunctions were rapidly giving way before a gathering tempest of scorn and resentment: 'what feelings are these that have come so inconveniently to light at this stage of the proceedings?   I have never heard of them before.'

'No,' said Olivia, 'I have done my best to conceal them from every one—from Mr. de Renzi, from you, from myself, unhappily, till now. Isabella, have compassion on me! I have been disgracefully weak. I ought to have refused him at first : but I wished for him, I wished to love him. I told him then, I told you, that I felt in doubt. That feeling of doubt has never ceased. It has grown deeper and deeper. Now it fills me with terror ; or rather, I doubt no more.'

'I cannot understand it,' said Mrs. Heriot; 'you have had a most happy courtship, surely —a devoted lover, a delightful one. What have you discovered ?'

'I told you,' said Olivia, 'that, somewhere in my nature, a Puritan was stowed away.'

'A Puritan!' cried the other, more and more lost in amazement; 'what does it mean ?'

'It means remorse, melancholy, terror, repentance, contempt for many of their

ambitions, hatred for many of their pleasures,
a dread of many things that they say and do
with a light heart.   It makes me unintelligible
to those who have not got the key ; unintelligible to myself sometimes.   For weeks past
I have lived in the midst of pleasures ; they
have been the saddest of my life.   Since Mr.
de Renzi released me I feel a burthen off my
soul.   It was crushing me.'

'And you really mean that for this—I do
not know what to call it—this fit of Method-
ism, you have thrown away your chance, your
splendid chance.'

'Seriously and finally,' said Olivia ; 'Mr.
de Renzi will, I am certain, never renew the
subject.   He released me, he forgave me.
That is why I say he has been so kind.'

'He released you!' cried Mrs. Heriot
aghast.   'Olivia, you are a most extraordinary
girl and a most ungrateful one!'

'No,' said Olivia.   'Believe me.   Mr. de
Renzi does not think so, nor I hope will you.'

Mrs. Heriot burst into a scornful laugh.

'It is worse than ingratitude. You have made a fool of me. I have been a good friend to you. I have devoted time, strength, money, all to your advancement in the world. I have helped you to a splendid match. Meanwhile you have been amusing yourself by deceiving us all.'

'Deceiving you?' cried Olivia, starting to her feet.

'Deceiving me, Valentine, Mr. de Renzi, everybody. What do you suppose I brought you to London for?'

'I thought it was out of kindness,' said Olivia. 'It was very kind of you. You have been my good friend, as you say. I cannot thank you enough. I am grieved, most grieved, to have vexed you.'

'Vexed me!' cried Mrs. Heriot; 'and you come now and talk nonsense about your Puritan—nonsense that a child would blush at. Puritan indeed! You are a proficient,

Olivia.   I have known many women who are
good hands at it, but you are the most
accomplished flirt I have ever come across.
You are a marvel.   All London will be
chattering about you this evening.   But I
will have no more of it.   I give you till to-
night to reconsider.'

'It is useless,' said Olivia, 'I have said
the last word.'

'And this is my last word,' said Mrs.
Heriot, passion and despair at last carrying
everything before them; 'you are a mad
woman, and your madness is of a dangerous
species.'

'Spare me,' said Olivia, rising and moving
towards the door; 'I am not feeling well.
You have been very kind to me in times
past.   I am grateful, most sincerely grateful
for your kindness.   But that gives you no
right to insult me now in my moment of trial.'

Mrs. Heriot—her cheek pale, her lips
tight drawn, her steely gray eyes flashing—

stood like a baffled fury. 'You remember what I said last night?'

'I remember it,' said Olivia; 'I will obey you.'

At this moment a servant announced that Dr. Crucible had called, and had sent up to know if Miss Hillyard was at home.

CHAPTER XLI

A FRIEND IN NEED

' Fain would I something say, yet to what end ?
Thou hast nor ear nor soul to apprehend
The sublime motion and high mystery
And serious doctrine of virginity.
And thou art worthy that thou should'st not know
More happiness than is thy present lot.
Enjoy your dear wit and gay rhetoric,
That hath so well been taught her dazzling fence,
Thou art not fit to hear thyself convinced.'

DR. CRUCIBLE'S daily arrival at the Museum
was a matter of absolute regularity. His
occasional absences were events, the solemnity
of which was emphasised by elaborate arrangements and formal notification. On this event-
ful Monday, however, without a note of warn-
ing, he failed to appear at his accustomed
hour. A class of students which had

assembled in the hope of enlightenment on the co-relation of Forces, waited, grumbled, and separated at last with muttered objurgations at their truant instructor's unexampled un-punctuality. When, several hours behind his time, the doctor put in an appearance, it was obvious that he was the victim of an agitation which not all his stoicism would enable him wholly to conceal. Something very unusual must, his alarmed subordinates surmised, have occurred to produce so marked a disturbance in the tranquil flow of Dr. Crucible's official life. Those who knew him, and did not know the potent forces that were at work, might well be lost in amazement. Was the doctor going out of his mind? or—what most of his friends would have considered much the same thing—was he going to be married? or what?

The truth was that Dr. Crucible had passed a most exciting morning. He was accustomed to pride himself on the well-adjusted existence of a philosopher ; but before he had finished breakfast a letter had arrived from Olivia which upset his philosophic equilibrium beyond all hopes of recovery. Olivia always touched him in a tender spot. Ever since her visit to Lady Heriot they had been sworn friends. He had protested against her alliance with Mrs. Valentine Heriot as a deplorable defection—a mistake from which rude experience would, sooner or later, awaken her. He denounced her engagement as the scandalous achievement of Mrs. Heriot's worldly contrivance. Olivia now wrote in great distress. Her letter seemed like a cry for pity—for help. She was in the most dreadful difficulty. She had at last, she said, after many searchings of heart, made up her mind that her engagement must be broken off. Every one would, she well knew, oppose her change of mind and condemn it ; and no wonder. No one would understand the cause. Mrs. Heriot especially, to whom

she was under great obligations, was furious
at the bare suggestion.   The prospect was
alarming.   There was a dreadful time before
her to go through, a dreadful battle to fight.
' I am alone ; I have no friend here ; I have
no adviser ; no one to sympathise ; no one to
help me.   Such friends as I have will all be
against me.   Isabella Heriot will be turned
from friend to foe.   I dread encountering her.
I am to be sent away unless I submit ; but I
can never submit.   Will you come and see
me ?'

The note of distress throughout the letter
was acute.   It moved the doctor to his heart's
core.   It appealed to all his paternal fondness
for Olivia ; but it did something more—it
filled him with the exultation of an ardent
warrior, who knows that the long-desired
moment of combat has at last arrived.   It
sounded a very tocsin in his ears.   It was a
trumpet-call for the assault—the assault that
he had so long panted to deliver, that he had

so often, in thoughts to which the wish was father, imagined himself delivering. Dr. Crucible did not like De Renzi. He cordially detested Mrs. Heriot. He had discussed all the story of the will with Lydia Hazelden, and unhesitatingly espoused her prejudices and convictions on the subject. He was satisfied that the codicil had been brought about by some infamous means, and that Isabella was the culprit. His old friend's last hours had been darkened, her real intentions defeated by this abandoned schemer. Sir Adrian's fortunes had received a mortal blow. His favourite, Jack, had been vilely ousted from his rights. The doctor's soul grew black whenever the subject crossed his thoughts. He predicted the most awful retribution on Mrs. Heriot's guilt. Metaphorically speaking, he thirsted for her blood. He would have liked to put his foot upon her neck—that much admired, much bedizened neck. His vengeance had hitherto been restricted to an impotent indulgence in abuse of the object of his wrath—calling her Canidia, Messalina, Borgia, and other evil names behind her back. But he was now to meet Canidia face to face. *Væ victis!* Dr. Crucible summoned a hansom, and drove away merrily for the battlefield, and arrived opportunely as the encounter between Mrs. Heriot and Olivia had reached that critical stage at which the intervention of a third party would turn the fortunes of the day.

CHAPTER XLII

STONEHOUSE DENOUNCES A JOB

'Avouons au moins que nous devons à l'infortune le plus
cher de nos rêves, celui du bonheur : car un sourire
n'est qu'une larme qui sèche : la joie n'est qu'un chagrin
qui se calme.'

THAT night Dr. Crucible and Stonehouse
were dining together at the Parthenon, and
Crucible, proud of his morning's achievement,
and of the possession of a really interesting
piece of gossip, lost no time in communicat-
ing it to his companion.

'Have you heard about De Renzi?' he
asked. 'His match with the young beauty
is broken off. You remember her two years
ago in Seymour Street?'

'Remember her?' said Stonehouse. 'Do

you think I am a stock-fish? I had the honour of taking her to the play—a charming girl, bright, clever, and good—too good for the De Renzis to smelt in their gold-pots. I hope that she is not broken-hearted about it?'

'Broken-hearted!' cried Crucible. 'It is *she* that has broken off the match. She found that she did not like him.'

Stonehouse poured out a glass of port with an air of mock solemnity.

'I drink to her good health. I applaud her courage; it is a courageous act.'

'I join in the toast,' said the doctor, gleefully replenishing his glass. 'If she cares about money, there are plenty of young plutocrats with as much fortune as De Renzi and a better reputation.'

'Yes,' said Stonehouse,

> "Uno avulso, non deficit alter
> Aureus, et simili frondescet virga metallo—"

The golden tree of London has a never-

failing supply of precious branches.   May
she find one to her taste!'

'I do not join in that,' said Crucible. 'For
my part, I should like her to marry her cousin,
Jack Heriot, who has been in love with her
ever since he was a lad.'

'Ah,' observed Stonehouse, 'but that won't
do.   Master Jack has got to put to something in the family pot.   If he wants to keep
Huntsham, he must find some of these golden
young ladies to keep house with—somebody
who, besides looking pretty, will pay his
butcher's and baker's bills for him.'

'Humph!' said the doctor; 'I should have
thought that the Heriots had had enough of
that sort of thing, with Valentine's experience and his stucco wife.   I saw that horrible
woman this morning.   She has pillage written
in her eyes—pillage and fury!   She fought
like a very dragon, but I rescued An-
dromeda.'

'And what have you done with her, now

that she is rescued?' asked Stonehouse.
'Your rescued heroine is apt to be embarrass-
ing to her deliverer. Have you got her on
the premises? Because, if so, I will come
home to tea with you.'

'Profane!' said Dr. Crucible. 'I have
handed her over to Mrs. Hazelden, who consented, like a good angel, to befriend her.
She needs a refuge and consolation. The
encounter with the dragon has shattered her.'

'And the loss of a lover!' said Stonehouse. 'But she will recover, you will see;
Andromedas of twenty generally do. How
delighted old Sir Raphael will be! Everybody will vow that he contrived it.'

'But about Jack Heriot now,' said Crucible; 'he cannot go on all his life playing
at art and socialism. It is not respectable.
Fancy a Heriot in a velveteen jacket with
his hair down his back!'

'We live in an epoch of revolution,' said
Stonehouse. 'If young Heriot chooses to let

down his back hair, I should not concern
myself.   The Spartans did it before their
battles.   Artists live and prosper nowadays.
They immortalise Lord Mayors and smart
ladies—they illustrate the magazines, and, I
observe, the advertisements.   Millais's boy is
for ever blowing Pears's soap-bubbles in my
face.   I am haunted, on my road to chambers
every morning, by a colossal atrocity, who
leers at me over several acres of naked
shoulder, amid a Niagara of golden hair.   I
daresay some fellow got well paid for painting her.   Why should not Jack make a living
at it ? '

'It is a Bohemian existence,' objected
Crucible.

'I like the Bohemians,' replied Stonehouse ; 'we want more of them.   Human
life is growing too precise.   We are all of
us infernal prigs.   Respectability, as some
one said of the Boston streets, stalks amongst
us unabashed.'

'Well,' said Crucible, 'the long and the short of it—if you will have it—is that I have another plan in my head for him. Should you be surprised to hear that Lord Melrose has carried his way with the Museum Commissioners, and that they have, at last, consented to allow me a librarian?'

'Stop!' cried Stonehouse; 'I refuse to listen. Thou corrupter of youth, thou jobber! Tell not your nefarious deeds of darkness to an honest man over his port.'

'A librarian,' continued Crucible, quite unabashed by the other's invective, '£500 a year, quarters in the Museum, and as many coals and candles as you please. The only difficulty is to find the proper man. Lord Melrose is good enough to leave the nomination entirely to me.'

'Well,' said Stonehouse, 'and what are the essentials of a librarian? Youth, ignorance, flightiness, to have thrashed a policeman, to be son of a broken-down baronet

and the lover of a pretty girl. Can such
a man be found? By the way, are you
sure that Jack Heriot can read? It is
desirable, I believe, that a librarian should
possess that accomplishment.'

'Read!' cried Crucible with scorn. 'A
librarian—*my* librarian, must have a touch
of genius; he must not be a pedant; he
must not be a bore; he must be young, or
he will not be malleable, and malleability
is indispensable; he must be a gentleman;
he must be a scholar; he must be a
university man, a cultured man, a com-
panionable man, with whom I can go and
chat about the books——'

'And,' said Stonehouse, 'he must have
a charming young wife, with whom you
can go and chat about the babies! Thou
double-dyed jobster, deem not that thou
wilt escape unscathed! A virtuous press
shall expose thy iniquity—a virtuous patriot,
one Stonehouse to wit, shall denounce

thee to a shuddering senate — " Quọsque
tandem, Crucibille, nostrâ abutere patientiâ ?"
Society——'

'Society,' said Crucible, 'will come to tea,
and talk about the babies. Providentially
there is a gallery, now wasted on fossils,
which can be cut up into a nursery when
the time arrives. I have arranged it
already.'

'Well,' said Stonehouse, 'it is a fortunate
thing for the young, amorous, and impro-
vident that there are some men who will
stick at nothing in the shape of crime—" Ces
amis de famille sont capables de tout." But
since you will do it, you may as well have
my blessing on the job. Have you told the
young person ?'

'Jack Heriot? I am to see him to-
morrow. As likely as not he will refuse it.'

'As likely as not,' said Stonehouse, 'he
will do nothing of the kind, especially when
he hears about the nurseries.'

'His first question,' Crucible said sententiously, 'will, I know, be as to his fitness for the post. He is excessively conscientious.'

'Of course,' said Stonehouse, 'that always is the first question with the lucky one whose friends job him into a sinecure. What a comfort that he is so fit! Once in harness, he will go straight enough, no doubt.'

'He will never go straight,' said Crucible, 'if by "straight" you mean humdrum; but he is none the worse for that! He will never be humdrum! He has ideas and aspirations of his own—a something in his head, a touch of poetry, a touch of originality. He is a nympholept! Sometime or other he has caught sight of an unearthly presence flitting through the forest glades, a glimpse of a white flowing skirt——'

'A glimpse of Olivia's petticoat,' cried Stonehouse with irreverent bursts of laughter.

'He'll catch her fast enough when once you have given him the place. Meantime, when the papers attack you, you can explain that he is a nympholept. It is a new apology.'

'And no bad one,' said Crucible. 'I am one of the old school in love matters, and believe that the best chance for a young fellow is to have an ideal—an ideal woman, and to be resolved to win her.'

'You are a nympholept yourself,' cried Stonehouse, 'and a match-maker to boot! I daresay you have already been conspiring with Master Jack.'

'Conspirators,' said Crucible with complacency, 'are not in the habit of disclosing their plots at their clubs after dinner. We shall see what will come of it.'

The truth was that Crucible had already written to Jack to come and see him, and the next morning that young gentleman, who had long found the doctor an excellent confidant, made his appearance at breakfast-time, and was skilfully prepared by his host for the fateful announcement. He was, as it happened, in the depths of low spirits.

' How goes the world with you, Jack, and your painting ?' the doctor asked. ' Is the masterpiece forthcoming ?'

' The masterpiece!' cried Jack disconsolately; 'I am just learning enough to know what masterpieces mean, and why it is that only one man in a million achieves one, and why I never should if I tried for a century. The fact is, doctor, to do anything respectable in art you must have genius. Few are the happy ones who possess it! I have not a touch of it. I can ride, I can shoot, I could dig if I got the chance, but paint I cannot. I can be nothing but a drudge, and the drudges are too numerous already. What does it matter? It is only one knock the more. I have had some hard ones, have I not? I have put a bold face on it, but, to tell you the truth, I feel rather beaten.'

'Never say die!' cried the doctor; 'you are not beaten yet, Jack, or within a hundred miles of it. Who knows when the luck will turn?'

'How can the luck turn for me?' said the other; 'and why should I care about its turning? I ought to care, I suppose; but I am hard hit, very hard. I went to see Olivia the other day, and take her my wedding offering. I have had a bad time since then. I ought not to have gone, but, like a fool, I went; I could not help it. I have paid dearly for my folly. I love her ten times more than ever. She was sweet to me. She spoke with tears in her eyes. I believe she is being forced into it. Aunt Valentine is forcing her. I am powerless to save her.'

'Well,' said the doctor, who considered that the proper moment for the revelation

had arrived, 'now I have something to tell
you. She has saved herself. She sent for
me yesterday about it. She has broken off
her engagement.'

'She has!' cried Jack, jumping up and
seizing the doctor's hand. 'Thank God for
that; and thank you for telling me. You
are sure? Aunt Isabella is a deep one.'

'You are right, Jack, your aunt is a deep
one. I had the satisfaction yesterday of
seeing her, for once, out of her depth. It is
a bad business for Olivia though, is it not?
What will become of her, poor girl?'

'Ah!' cried Jack, flushing hot with excitement and already on the sunny pinnacles of
hope; 'but she is well out of that business, at
any rate. It was Canidia's contrivance. I
saw it all along. She would never have
been happy. I know him and I know her.
It would have been an unhappy marriage.'

'Well,' said the doctor, 'she is resolved,
at any rate, not to make the experiment.

She is not likely to get another chance of making it again in a hurry. Young millionaires and rising statesmen are not to be had for the asking. De Renzi is an enormous catch.'

'De Renzi,' cried Jack, 'is a—but no; he is a trump—an angel for letting her find him out in time and for giving her a lesson. He will have sickened her of wealth.'

'Who knows?' said the doctor, who was not incapable of a teasing mood; 'perhaps she has a still richer man in her eye. Girls have done such things before now.'

'You know she has nothing of the sort,' cried Jack; 'she is as good as gold.'

'She means to be a duchess,' said his persecutor; 'I am convinced. Why not? There are several young marquesses available. She wants a dukedom.'

'She wants a fiddlestick!' cried Jack. 'She has not defied Aunt Isabella and all her works for that.'

' But now for business,' said Crucible ; ' I did not send for you to discuss Olivia's love affairs.'

' Did you not ? ' cried Jack, who at that moment was incapable of fancying anything else in the world that could so well deserve discussion. ' Then what did you want me for ? '

' I want you for business,' said the doctor, ' a business matter of importance. I want your assistance. I have a post to give away. I have been commissioned to look out for a librarian for the Museum. The work will be heavy ; the salary is small ; £500 a year and quarters in the building. Probably only a man devoted to science for its own sake would be prepared to make the sacrifice of accepting it. Can you help me to a choice ? '

Jack went away presently, the happiest, hopefullest young fellow in London. The luck had turned indeed. His troubles were forgotten. Life lay before him, rosy with delightful possibilities. The world had suddenly grown bright. Hope flooded the scene with golden rays. Olivia was free. Olivia might yet be won. 'Never say die,' indeed! No one of all the thousands of stalwart lads, who hurried through London's streets that morning to their daily task at the great wheel of life, felt less like saying it.

A week later Jack was established at the Museum in a wilderness of learned volumes, and had set himself manfully to the task of reducing them to order. Crucible took him over the Museum and explained to him the geography of his new home.

'What is this?' asked the new librarian, as they passed into a long gallery, to which piles of fossils, heaped about in chaotic profusion, gave a neglected air. 'Is this part of my kingdom?'

'Not at present,' said the doctor; 'these are some palæozoic friends of mine, and have no business here at all.   I intend to replace them by some of the more recent mammals. Some day, if the librarian should be a married man, and should happen to require it, this will be the nursery.'

CHAPTER XLIII

DR. CRUCIBLE AS A DIPLOMATIST

' I cannot love him ;
Yet I suppose him virtuous, know him noble,
Of great estate, of just and stainless youth,
In voices well divulged, free, learned, valiant,
And in dimension and the shape of nature
A gracious person : but yet I cannot love him ;
He might have took his answer long ago.'

No one ever knew, for Crucible refused to divulge them, the details of the encounter between Mrs. Heriot and himself. It is certain, however, that the doctor stood to his guns like a man, undeterred by Mrs. Heriot's wrath, and that the battle ended in his carrying off Olivia in triumph to his chambers in the Albany. Having established his guest in such comfort as bachelor quarters allow, the doctor started off to Mrs. Hazelden's to enlist that lady's assistance in disposing of his guest.

Dr. Crucible had need of all his diplomacy and all the weight of an old-standing family friendship when he essayed to induce Mrs. Hazelden to give Olivia a refuge. She came from a suspicious quarter—a deserter from the enemy's camp. Of all houses in London her sister-in-law's was the last to which Mrs. Hazelden would naturally have gone to find a friend or a dependant. Isabella, if she was nothing worse, was the incarnation of vulgar smartness. She was showy, she was worldly, she was unscrupulous; everything, in fact, that a young girl's guardian ought not to be. She had adopted Olivia, and given her a couple of years of her precious advice and example.

'Olivia,' Mrs. Hazelden now said decisively, 'must by this time be completely spoilt.'

'I tell you,' said the doctor gallantly, 'that nothing could spoil her, not even such a chaperon as Mrs. Heriot. Does her behaviour look like it? She is as good now as she was two years ago, when your mother was so fond of her.'

'I have no time for maidens all forlorn,' said Mrs. Hazelden; 'no time and no taste. They are quite out of my line. I don't like love affairs, unsuccessful ones least of all. I should not know what to do with her.'

'But what am *I* to do with her?' pleaded Crucible. 'You cannot leave a young creature like that to shift for herself.'

'She will flirt with my boys,' said Mrs. Hazelden. 'She will turn their foolish heads, as once upon a time she turned poor Jack's.'

'Happily,' said the doctor, 'the big ones are away, and the little ones are too little to be in any danger; but she will teach them as much Greek and Latin as you please.'

'If she can do that she will be a bene-
factress!' cried Mrs. Hazelden; 'it is more
than I can do. They are idle little rascals,
spoilt with soft living and too many holidays.
As for learning anything, they cannot even
spell their mother tongue.'

'Olivia will soon put that to rights.
Spelling is one of her strong points. She
has so many.'

'A first-rate champion among the rest,'
said Mrs. Hazelden. 'She is a paragon, no
doubt; but paragons are troublesome in-
mates. Why should I undertake her?'

'Why?' cried Crucible. 'Because, my
dear lady, she is in trouble and needs your
help, and deserves it. Your mother loved
her; she would have rejoiced to help her.
Do as she would have done. Show what
you think of Isabella Heriot's proceeding in
turning her adrift. I can conceive nothing
that she would dislike so much as that you
should harbour Olivia just now.'

'Then I will certainly do so,' said Mrs. Hazelden, pleased to find a cross-grained excuse for a good-natured act; 'you may bring her when you please.'

'You are a good woman!' cried Crucible, seizing her hand; 'your mother's true daughter. I will go and bring her to you at once. God bless you for helping her!'

.   .   .   .   .

Olivia soon satisfied her hostess that she had not been spoilt. She carried herself bravely, and betrayed not the slightest symptom of being broken-hearted. No one could have worn less of the air of the maiden all forlorn. She set to work in real earnest with the two small boys, who were at home for the holidays, and who speedily declared themselves ready to do anything, even vulgar fractions and dictation, that Olivia wished. Mrs. Hazelden, after holding her at arm's length for some days, at last threw away her suspicions and began to grow confidential.

Olivia found herself surprised into the awful topic of her engagement.

'Do you think I was excessively to blame?' Olivia ventured, with some trepidation, to inquire.

'Excessively,' said Mrs. Hazelden; 'you have let a fine fortune slip out of your fingers, and spoilt one of Isabella's plans! How can I forgive you? But, seriously, Olivia, do you wish to know what I think about you?'

'Yes,' said Olivia; 'that is, if it will do me good to know it. But remember, please, that I am in need of consolation, not reproach. I can do that for myself.'

'Well,' said Mrs. Hazelden, suddenly growing serious, 'I will tell you. If my esteem, Olivia, my warm regard, my hearty sympathy and approval will console you, you may be consoled. Do I think you to blame, indeed? Do I think courage to blame, and reason, and honour, and the brave resolve to

save yourself, at whatever cost, from a life of
unhappiness and turpitude?'

'Turpitude!' cried Olivia.

'It is a strong word,' said the other, 'is it
not? but none too strong for the lives that
women like Isabella Heriot lead,—their
aims, their motives, their pleasures. She
wanted to make them yours, Olivia. Your
peril was great. I rejoice to think that you
have escaped. You are meant for better
things; they will come in due time.'

'You are a good consoler,' said Olivia,
laying her hand fondly on Mrs. Hazelden's;
'some of the good things have come already.
I feel stronger and better for my life with
you. I am happy here. You will always be
my friend, will you not?'

'Always,' said Mrs. Hazelden, 'so long
as you do not make friends with the
mammon of unrighteousness. When you
do that, you will have to give me up. The
mammon of unrighteousness of our day is, to

my taste, bad of its kind—sordid, despicable,
to be abhorred.   You have seen it ; you
know enough.'

'I know enough,' said Olivia, 'to wish to
know no more.   Isabella preached me a
rough lesson.'

'A rough lesson,' said the other, 'and a
wholesome one.   She is a sermon in herself,
a brilliant instance, a true daughter of her
age—the age of self-indulgence.'

CHAPTER XLIV

VETERIS VESTIGIA FLAMMÆ

'But besides those, who make good in our imagination the place of Muses and of Delphic sibyls, are there not women who fill our vase with wine and roses to the brim, so that the wine runs over and fills the house with perfume: who inspire us with courtesy; who unloose our tongues and we speak; who anoint our eyes and we see? We say things we never thought to have said; for once our walls of reserve vanished, and left us at large; we were children playing with children in a wide field of flowers. "Steep us," we cried, "in these influences for days and weeks, and we shall be sunny poets, and will write out in many-coloured words the romance that you are."'

WHETHER Mr. Emerson's high-flown description of the charming woman's influences on human nerves and brain was a day-dream of his own poetic temperament, or is a veracious portraiture of processes which actually occur among mortals, is a question which, for obvious reasons, it is expedient to leave undetermined. Few men, certainly, are known to their contemporaries to go about in this ecstatic plight with loosened tongues and bliss-anointed eyes, crying out to be steeped in celestial influences. But then it is possible that the women, capable of producing such delicious enthralment, may also be few. That such women exist, is certain. Every man probably knows one at least, and tastes differ. M. Sainte Beuve, who ought to know, declares it to be impossible to write about women without first putting oneself in a good humour by thinking of Madame de Sévigné. Madame de Sévigné's husband, on the other hand, did not care about her. Rousseau, at the time he was firing the sentiment of Europe, declared his Theresa delightful, despite her dirt, ignorance, and stupidity ; as afterwards, no doubt, did Theresa's second lord, the congenial stable-boy. Be this as it may, Jack Heriot was enthralled. Olivia was his muse, his sibyl, his inspiring genius, his all-dominating influence. When he was with her, his rose-crowned cup ran over with bliss. When he left her, he carried away an enchanted memory. The only drawback was that the period of existence, during which he had to content himself with the pleasures of memory, was so vastly in excess of that in which the actual fruition of his adored one's presence was vouchsafed. Olivia was but seldom to be seen. His aunt's door was not open to him with the ready hospitality of other times.

'Now, Jack,' Mrs. Hazelden had said in her brusque fashion, 'don't you be coming here too often; I cannot have idle boys about the house.'

'I am not an idle boy,' said Jack, 'but a studious man—tremendously studious.'

'And so is Olivia,' said his aunt; 'she is busy with the children's lessons and her own,

I should hope.   She is trying to catch up all
the time your aunt has made her work.   She
wishes to study.'

'Yes,' said Jack, 'I have seen her study-
ing—

> "a student air,
> With a look half sad, half saintly,
> Grave sweet eyes, and flowing hair"—

Aunt Lydia, don't be hard upon me.   I am
a fool.   I cannot help it.   She is a woman
to worship.'

'Jack, dear fellow,' said his aunt, looking
at him with kindly, compassionate eyes,
'take my advice, and don't come here too
often, and, still more, don't be too affec-
tionate, "Chi va lento, va sano : chi va sano,
va lontano"—one false step and you will
spoil your chance.'

'Then,' said Jack, catching at the first
straw which offered, 'you think I have a
chance?'

'No,' said his aunt, 'I did not mean that.

I meant that you may make it impossible that you ever should have one. I came upon a good remark somewhere the other day which I commend to you, namely, that men are slow, in their conceit, to recognise what a valuable ally in their love-making they might make of distance. It lends enchantment to the view.'

'Distance!' cried Jack. 'That is a bitter remedy.'

'Most good remedies are,' said his aunt. 'If you want her, Jack, go the right way about it, and begin by not being in a hurry! Olivia is in no mood just now for love-making. Come when I ask you. You do really want her, don't you?'

'Want her!' cried Jack, who was by this time perfectly incapable of talking rationally on the subject—'Want her! Ah, Aunt Lydia, if you only knew how much, and for how long I have wanted her! You must help me, will you not?'

'Well,' said his aunt, 'I am helping you now, when I tell you to make yourself reasonably scarce, and not to waste my mornings and hers. Ah, there is the bell! As you are here, I must, I suppose, allow you to stay for lunch.'

It had always been part of Jack's boyish creed that, despite her austerity of doctrine, his Aunt Lydia was, *au fond*, 'a brick.' Never had he more heartily subscribed to that belief than now; and while he was still mentally blessing her, Olivia came in from a walk in the park with the children, looking like a young goddess—fresh, radiant, beautiful, raining her genial influences in generous profusion on all around her—firing Jack's young blood, filling his heart with a thrill of admiration, a rush of eager desire and hope. 'Want her?' 'Wait for her?' Live for her, die for her! What was he not ready to do, to dare, to suffer, if only this fair creature might one day be his!

One practical step towards the accomplishment of his happiness it was open to Jack to take forthwith. It was a relief to take it. When he went, next day, to Huntsham to tell his parents of the good fortune which, by Crucible's intervention, had befallen him, Lady Eugenia thought it incumbent on her, as a good mother, to improve the occasion by renewing the suggestion which she had often heretofore made in vain—that Jack's way to comfort and happiness lay in the direction of a judicious marriage. She had several young ladies on her list, all of whom she considered eligible. Jack, she was convinced, as became a partial mother, could not fail to be a welcome wooer. Now, too, besides an agreeable person and a prospective baronetcy, Jack had the additional recommendation of a respectable official post to offer to the destined sharer of his affections. It seemed more than ever equitable that the young lady honoured by

Jack's selection should, on her part, bring an equivalent in the shape of solid wealth.

'It is what everybody has to do,' Lady Eugenia said ; 'what, in fact, everybody not born to a fortune does. How else, I should like to know, is a gentleman to live ? '

Lady Eugenia, in numberless communings with her own heart on the subject, had convinced herself that no satisfactory answer could be given to this question, and, accordingly, that her point was proved. It was a surprise, a mortification now to find that it carried no conviction to Jack's too stubborn understanding.

'How is a gentleman to live ? ' he said in disrespectful tones. 'By earning a livelihood, like an honest man, or, if he cannot do that, by going without it. Worse things might happen.'

'Well,' said Lady Eugenia, her armoury of argument fairly exhausted, 'you do not suppose you can live on £500 a year, do you ? '

'Why not?' cried Jack. 'Anyhow, I mean to try, and to get Olivia to try with me, if I can. Do not talk to me, please, about any other girl. I don't care a straw for one of them; it is Olivia or nobody for me. I have waited a long time, mother; I have done all that you and father asked me; now you must take my part. I can never give her up.'

Lady Eugenia was an easy conquest, and once conquered became a vigorous ally. Sir Adrian showed more obduracy. His mind was difficult to move. He hated the idea of Olivia as a daughter-in-law. She had gone over to the enemy. Such a defection was unforgivable. She had joined Isabella Heriot, had become her dependant, had accepted her favours, and had, no doubt, imbibed her principles. Who could tell what baneful arts, what vile and dangerous secrets that abandoned worldling might not have taught her? Her engagement to De Renzi implied a sordid ambition, her breach of it a

fickle temper. Sir Adrian committed himself
more and more zealously to the task of
proving that Olivia could never make a
decent wife. He disparaged her good looks.
There were too many good-looking women,
he protested, whose husbands had the worst
of the bargain. Then Jack flew into a
passion and declined to discuss the subject
any more. The crisis was unprecedented in
the family annals. Jack and his father had
never had a real quarrel before, and this
quarrel was a desperate one. Jack was in an
implacable mood. His father's rough phrases
had stung him to the quick. He would never,
Lady Eugenia felt certain, give in. Could
it be expected that he should? Many evil
things had befallen Sir Adrian, but that his
son should leave the house in open rebellion!
What might not happen next?

Lady Eugenia betook herself nervously to
the delicate task of reconciliation; but Sir
Adrian was not easy to be reconciled.

'She is Isabella's *protégée*, her creature,' he said in stubborn tones,—' Isabella, my worst enemy and Jack's.'

'She has broken with Isabella,' cried his wife; 'she has given up everything sooner than submit to her schemes. What could she do more? Lydia, who is a good wife, you will admit, is delighted with her. Pray, Adrian, do not put yourself in the wrong with the best, the most loyal son that ever lived. Life would be unendurable to me.'

The result of Lady Eugenia's diplomacy was that Jack succeeded in obtaining his father's consent to his engagement, and that, a few days later, several luggage-vans were despatched, loaded with a goodly supply of Chippendale chairs and tables, which had been for years wasting their sweetness in the lumber-rooms of Huntsham, and were now destined for the embellishment of Jack's quarters in the Museum. Sir Adrian was reconciled to the idea of Olivia as a daughter-in-law. It had been decreed in the family councils that Jack was now to become a married man as soon as the Fates, who sway the female heart, permitted that delightful consummation. Everything now depended on the Fates and on Olivia.

CHAPTER XLV

' Of all the paths which lead to woman's heart,
Pity's the straightest.'

OLIVIA had now for a year had her home at Mrs. Hazelden's. The silent flow of un-eventful months, none of which brought change or cheerfulness to the situation, was at last interrupted by a crisis, sufficiently acute to mark a new departure. One day Mrs. Hazelden came into Olivia's room in unusual excitement, with a letter in her hand. ' I have had agitating news this morning,' she said. ' A purchaser has been found for Huntsham ; in a few days, my brother writes, the sale will be completed. If I wish to visit

my old home once more, I must go at once.
I mean to go to-day, to say good-bye to the
place I love best on earth. I am weak about
it, I know, Olivia ; but it grieves me to the
quick. It is hard on us all. It has been a
dear, dear home. I love it more than I knew
I did, more, I suppose, than a reasonable being
ought ; anyhow, it is going !'

'And Jack !' cried Olivia ; 'he will mind
it dreadfully. What a sacrifice ! He was
right to do it, was he not ? but how hard it
seems !'

'He was right,' said Mrs. Hazelden, 'if
the honest, the chivalrous thing is the right
one, which sometimes I begin to doubt.
Jack is chivalrous to the core—the soul of
honour. Such men come off badly in the
world. Fancy him and his father without a
home !'

The tears stood in Mrs. Hazelden's eyes.
Her lips trembled. She spoke in broken
tones. She was greatly moved. Olivia had

never seen this sturdy woman so little
mistress of herself. For once her habitual
stoicism failed her.

'It is cruel for you all,' said Olivia,
sitting down by her companion; 'a dreadful
loss. I can share it. I have such pleasant
memories of Huntsham. What happy visits
I have paid there as a child! It was there
the great good fortune of my life befell me—
Lady Heriot's friendship.'

'Dear mother!' said Mrs. Hazelden; 'it
is well that she is in her grave. It would
have broken her heart. She loved the old
place. How fond she was of you, Olivia!'

'She was very good to me,' said Olivia;
'my life with her was delightful; it is
delightful to remember. How happy my
father used to be with Sir Adrian! Ah,
if one could only have those dear people,
those happy days again!'

'Come, come,' cried Mrs. Hazelden, 'do
not let us be sentimental. I must go about

my housekeeping. My train goes at twelve.
What is the good of looking back? As
for you, Olivia, you are too young for such
wishes. You must look forward. Life is
full of promise to you—promise of happiness.
You are happy here, are you not?'

'Most happy,' said Olivia, with emphasis
—'most happy, and most grateful to the
best of friends. I should be a wretch if I
were not. Yet I am often sad, I do not
know why. I miss my father dreadfully:
no one can ever be what he was to me.
Sometimes I think my loss grows worse
to me as time goes on. Now you are in
trouble; it grieves me. Life is a bad
bnsiness, is it not?'

'No,' said Mrs. Hazelden, getting up
resolutely and turning to Olivia as she
prepared to leave the room, 'not to the
young, the hopeful, the courageous. Take
courage, Olivia, I prophesy a life of happiness for you.'

'Kind prophetess!' said Olivia; 'you fulfil your own prophecy. You give me what you promise. But when you are sad I must be sad too.'

Mrs. Hazelden stood looking at Olivia for some seconds, with eyes of tender scrutiny, as if debating something with herself. Then her resolution was formed. 'Would you like to come with me to Huntsham?' she said; 'you may if you will. It is a family gathering. We shall like to have you.'

'But'—said Olivia in hesitating tones——

'You need feel no "buts,"' said Mrs. Hazelden; 'I have an express invitation to you from Eugenia.'

'You have?' cried Olivia, to whom this intelligence seemed—she had not time to think why—to stir a slumbering world of thoughts within her to sudden life. 'I should like it above everything. You are sure that I shall not be in the way?'

'I am sure,' said Mrs. Hazelden; 'you will be welcome, Olivia, most welcome—the last guest the Heriots will ever have in their old home. It is cruel to take you. It will be a dismal scene.'

'Then,' said Olivia, 'I will share it with you. Let me come.'

The scene at Huntsham was, in truth, sufficiently dismal. However much we discount our troubles by anticipation, their actual arrival has a grimness of its own. Sir Adrian had been for years dreaming about the sale of Huntsham, talking about it, preparing the way for it. He had figured it a hundred times in fancy, but he had never known how much it would cost him to realise it in actual fact. He was now dreadfully cast down, too dejected to maintain the outward semblance of cheerfulness or to ignore the disaster which was befalling himself and his household. The Heriots, as a family, were ended. The house which

had been their home, the outward and
visible sign of all that an old family means,
the centre of so many interests, the symbol
of so many sentiments, was to pass away—
its soul extinct, its traditions outraged, its
poetry forgotten—to a strange owner, who
would regard it simply as so much mere
brick and mortar, the equivalent of so many
thousand pounds—whose only questions
about it would be whether he had bought
it sufficiently cheap, and how it might be
best improved. Sir Adrian's soul sank in
sorrow and abasement at the thought. The
blow had fallen at last. It was in vain to
dissimulate ; it was a disaster.

Olivia was greatly impressed by all she
saw at Huntsham. The heroism of these
good, brave people, the framework of whose
outer life seemed crumbling all around them
—their dignity, their calmness, their submission struck her as noble, pathetic. It
had an almost tragic grandeur, a tragic

sadness. Sir Adrian, in the midst of his troubles, showed all the fine courtesy of his earlier days. He was awaiting them in the hall as the carriage drove up, as picturesque, as striking a figure as any of the older generations of Heriots who graced the walls around him. He looked, Olivia thought, the ideal of a brave gentleman amid the blows of fate, whose fortunes are at a low ebb, but whose honour is unstained, his fortitude unshaken. Trouble had told upon him. His hair had grown white: some lines of care were written on his brow, his form was somewhat bent, as of one who bowed beneath life's heavy burthen. He looked grave, broken, sad; but he was gentleness itself. Olivia felt the tears rush to her eyes as he held her hand and bade her welcome. 'You have grown very like your mother,' he said, 'and you have your father's eyes! Poor Hillyard, I wish I had him here just now! I am glad, at any rate,

to have his child.' Lady Eugenia was as
tender to Olivia as in old times, more
tender, perhaps. Her kiss of welcome had
a special warmth, as if it meant to convey
a message of love. The house was in
some disorder, for the arrangements for
dismantling it were already in hand, but
Olivia's comforts as a guest were well
provided for. 'You are to have your old
room, Olivia,' Lady Eugenia said, as they
went upstairs. 'I thought you would like
it. I will come with you. How sweet the
garden looks from the window, does it not?
The little girls have decked the table with
flowers in honour of our dear guest.'

The room seemed just as she remembered
it years before. Everything was so familiar,
so dear, so sad. Every one was being kind
to her. Olivia's heart was full.

Jack, whom they found when they went
to dinner, played his part manfully. He
behaved to his father with deference, and

surrendered without a struggle to arguments which at another time would have stirred the combatant within him. But Jack's heart was too sore to wrangle. Sir Adrian remained master of an undisputed field. Lady Eugenia found herself being delightfully cared for. Jack was always petting her. No one who had watched him would have guessed that he had signed away his heritage, and was in the act of losing it.

The occasion, Olivia felt, was one which justified outspokenness. How, at such a time, amid such friends, lock up one's real feelings, and check the natural, spontaneous flow of sympathy and kindness? All hearts were aching with a common sorrow. Each was feeling for the rest. Each wished to lighten his companion's load. In such an atmosphere it is difficult, it would be incongruous, not to become confidential. Olivia was longing to help, to cheer, to console. Who could stand in need of greater consola-

tion than Jack did, or could better deserve
to be consoled ?   Olivia, with pardonable
disregard of all but the necessities of the
moment, devoted herself to the congenial
task of consolation.   Lady Eugenia fanned
the flame.   Jack was no longer a forbidden
topic in her talks with Olivia.   She was
fervent in her praises of his unselfishness.
His mother might well be proud of such a
son.   She stood on the terrace one morning,
her eyes full of tears, watching Jack, his
father leaning on his arm, as they strolled
beneath the lime trees.   ' He is the best of
sons,' she said, ' and the best of men.   The
misfortune is his far more than ours.   Our
day is nearly done.   We have lived our
lives here.   But for Jack ! see how he takes
it !   I set him against a thousand misfortunes
and am thankful.'   In such a mood, could
Olivia show reluctance when, morning after
morning, Jack tempted her to come with him
and visit many a familiar spot, dear to the

recollections of them both ? Together they
wandered across the park, and through the
woods, and down to the little stream which
had formed the boundary of their childhood's
rambles.   It was sad, but yet a pleasant sort
of sadness.   Here they had played as boy
and girl.   Here was the elm which Jack, in
school-boy pride, had climbed to perilous
heights, while Olivia stood below in awe-
struck admiration at her companion's prowess.
Here was the lane where they had wasted so
many delicious afternoons ! Wasted, indeed !
What afternoons in after-life had ever been,
could ever be, half as well employed ? for
were they not fragrant still with a thousand
pleasant associations, and tuneful with sweet
sounds that it was a joy to remember ?

Olivia felt a tender pity take possession
of her soul.   It clamoured for expression.
She would be prude no longer.   She would
tell the truth ; she would say what she was
feeling — be the consequences what they

might. Jack, charmed with Olivia's melting
mood, was busy with a hundred pleasant
memories. 'Those were good days, Olivia,'
he cried, 'were they not? too good to last
or to return.   They come but once in a
lifetime, people tell us; well, it is something
to have had them once. They were the
happiest of my life.'

'And of mine,' said Olivia, by this time
in no mood to weigh her words; 'I have
never been so happy since. I am often sad
now—very sad to-day, Jack, because of your
troubles. I have wanted to tell you. You
bear it nobly.'

'You make them easy to bear,' said Jack;
'you are the best of consolers, the best and
the kindest. Despite of everything, you
have made these last days at Huntsham
very happy ones. I shall never forget
them.'

Olivia went back to the house a happy
woman—happier, more at peace, than she

had ever felt. Things around her looked gloomy, but an inward voice was whispering to her to be of good cheer. Happiness for her, for Jack, was close at hand. The night was dark; but already the horizon was beginning to glow with rosy harbingers of coming dawn. The occasion was a sad one, romantically sad: her dear friends were suffering; but Olivia had become conscious of something which forbade her to be sad, which filled her soul with joy, exultation, rapture—something which she had resolutely thrust away from sight and buried deep in the recesses of her heart. Now it would be ignored no more. There was no doubt this time, no misgiving, no room for hesitation. She had found the man she loved!

How smoothly, in such circumstances, does the course of wooing flow! How easy to reveal that which it has cost so much effort, so much suffering to hide, even, if possible, from oneself! What bootless effort,

what unnecessary pain! That evening, as
Jack and Olivia wandered about the moss-
grown Huntsham paths, and watched the
last lights of a sweet June day fading out of
the sky, how natural it seemed that, almost
before they knew, Jack's long-cherished
passion should find utterance, and that
Olivia should need but gentle compulsion to
own that he was master of her heart. It
was the old story of their childhood over
again—deeper, stronger, sweeter than before.
'I have had the heart-ache for a dozen
years!' cried Jack ; 'now, come what mishaps
may, I am the happiest of men, the happiest,
the most fortunate! How often I have
walked about these woods, building castles
in the air, or oftener railing against Fortune
because my castle would not build itself the
way I wished! I used to love to dream that
this dear old place would, one day, be your
home. It seemed a sort of consecration
of it.'

'I too have had day-dreams and a heart-
ache,' said Olivia; 'I have been miserable,
sometimes, and hopeless. I am thankful
that that part of life is done. I tried to
believe that happiness could be found elsewhere than where my heart bade me find it.
Now, at last, I am perfectly happy—happy
and at peace.'

The sun had set; the west was all aglow
with a soft dying glory; one star after
another looked out faintly from a darkening
sky; the exquisite dewy cool of summer
evening was falling on meadow and woodland, refreshing the world after the long
day's blaze. A nightingale was pouring out
a full flood of song from the neighbouring
thicket. All things seemed at peace, best
peace of all in two young lovers' hearts, to
whom the world has suddenly become a
palace of enchantment. 'My true life,' cried
Jack, as they turned homewards, 'begins
to-night—

" The last step has brought me to my love,
    And there I'll rest, as, after much turmoil,
    A blessed soul doth in Elysium "—

See, there is my father. Let us go and tell
him.'

It was not, however, destined that the
pleasant announcement should be made just
then. Sir Adrian met them with a troubled
face. 'I have had very bad news from your
Uncle Valentine,' he said; 'Antinous is
dangerously ill.'

CHAPTER XLVI

THE BEGINNING OF TROUBLES

'Though the mills of God grind slowly,
Yet they grind exceeding small.'

THINGS were going badly with Valentine and
his wife. Isabella Heriot was beginning to
find that the pleasures of life were fast losing
their flavour. Its excitements would stimu-
late no longer. With the ill-gotten wealth
that her mother-in-law's codicil had brought,
leanness had entered into her soul, leanness
and bitterness—the leanness of satiated desire,
the bitterness of disappointed hope. Society
had no more to give her in the way of enjoyment. She had climbed as high as she
could go, and found no such rapture as

that which she had looked up to from below.
Rather the air was harsh, the breeze chilly, the
mountain-side steep and slippery; it was
hard to advance, easy to fall. In a long list
of acquaintances, whose acquisition had cost
her so many days and nights of toil, Isabella
Heriot told herself bitterly that she had not
a single friend. Her husband was less to her
than ever. He had never forgiven her the
estrangement from his brother which her
behaviour had occasioned. Valentine in his
earlier days had wished for the money, he
had wanted it. He now wanted reconciliation with his brother and his family. The
estrangement was costing him more than he
had bargained for. Sir Adrian's haughty
politeness, when, once or twice, they had met
for business matters, cut him to the quick.
Huntsham was a closed house to him and his
wife. His sister Lydia would have nothing
to do with either of them. Many of
Valentine's friends, too, espoused Sir Adrian's

side, and looked coldly on Isabella's fine
dinners and crowded receptions. For himself, Valentine was thoroughly tired of them
and of Isabella too. He had known from the
first that she was a bad companion for a *tête-à-
tête*. There was no love, no pretence of
love; and the feelings which had once done
duty for love had turned to something near
dislike. So Valentine and his wife went
their different ways with exterior politeness
to each other, but each with a secret resentment, each with ever-lessening esteem, each
with hearts which daily grew darker and
colder, as new incongruities came to light and
indifference ripened into hate. He made no
secret of his dulness, and a dull man easily
becomes morose. If he frequented parties as
assiduously as ever, it was not that they
amused him, but because husband and wife
had accepted the bitter truth that anything
was better than one another's society.
Valentine had learnt to think of his home

with a shudder, for there—close by the sacred hearth, at the household table, beside the nuptial couch—sat the dread demon of *ennui*, master of the situation.

Another source of disturbance to Mrs. Heriot's domestic peace was the fact, which became daily more apparent, that Malcolm's health was breaking down. Little Antinous was fast approaching the age when he would require a more educated companion. But the idea of Malcolm quitting the household altogether had never been entertained. She was devoted to the child, and he to her. It would have been cruelty to separate them; and cruelty to Antinous was to Mrs. Heriot an unimaginable crime. The child, always her idol, became dearer to her as other pleasures lost their charm. He, at least, never disappointed; his mother found in his increasing attractions a balm for all her disappointments. Malcolm managed him better than any one. Nor was this all. Her

strength of character, her Puritanic earnest-
ness, her Scotch piety, her strong unswerving
loyalty to Mrs. Heriot, her impassioned
affection for the child, her long services, ex-
tending back to the days when Isabella was
a girl—gave her a special position in the
household, made her a privileged person.
She did many things for Antinous which his
mother was glad to be excused from doing.
She taught him her own gloomy creed ; she
talked to him of the things which fascinate
and awe a child's imagination ; she bade him,
above all things, be sure that his heart was
right with God, his conscience free from sin.
The child spent his life with her, for Mrs.
Heriot's plan of existence left little leisure for
the sort of intercourse which children need,
nor had she any aptitude for it.   No one in
the Heriot household could fill Malcolm's
place ; and now it was obvious that she was
failing.   Once the calmest, most composed,
most imperturbable of mortals, going her

way, unmoved by external influences, she was
now the victim of moods, or, rather, of one
despairing mood.   A profound melancholy
had settled upon her ; she was never happy,
never cheerful ; she went about her business
as in a day-dream ; her physical powers grew
daily less.   Her nerves were shattered ; she
had become an old woman.   Mrs. Valentine
watched her and made up her mind that she
was the victim of some mortal disease.
Doctors, however, failed to discover any
cause, and could indicate nothing more
distinct than want of tone.   Malcolm took
her tonics submissively, protested that there
was nothing the matter with her but old age,
and grew pale and haggard, as though the
Furies were driving her to her doom.

It was a fine June ; the heat was great.
London glowed like a spent furnace ;
Antinous began to flag.   He was pale, listless,
and evidently required country air.   Valentine
was tied to the City.   Mrs. Heriot had

various engagements which she] did not
choose to miss. Nurse and child accordingly
were despatched to Mrs. Heriot's home,
where Antinous was always a welcome guest.
There he was to await his parents' arrival for
a summer visit. Valentine was sharing a
moor with some friends, and in the middle of
August they would all start for Scotland.

Malcolm was thankful to escape to the
country. The heat and airlessness of London
was killing her. She longed for cool and
quiet. She would get better now, she felt.
The dewy, noiseless nights at the Pines, the
great vault of heaven slowly, in majestic
silence, wheeling overhead, were the remedy
of which she stood in need. Her parents
were still alive, privileged pensioners in one
of Mr. Goldingham's model cottages. Her
sister Maggie had just returned from India
and was now at home, a married woman with
a little child. Malcolm longed to be with her
kinsfolk once again; she wept passionately

as she threw herself into her old mother's arms. Maggie was horrified at her sister's looks. The sturdy, self-contained, determined woman was gone. She was but the wreck of her former self.

It was a blazing summer. There was nothing to be done but to sit in the shade under the beech trees in the park. Here Maggie would come with her little son, and the two women would sit chatting while the children played about together, Antinous perfectly happy in having found that supreme desideratum of childhood, a playmate. One day Antinous complained of thirst; the two children asked to be allowed to go to the cottage for a drink of water. It was against rules to go into any of the cottages, but old Malcolm's cottage was proverbial for its spotless purity. He himself, a hale old man of eighty, was a standing proof of the absence of every unhealthy influence. It was but a hundred yards from where they sate. The children begged hard and Malcolm gave them leave to go.

Antinous presently came back refreshed and delighted. Old Malcolm had received him hospitably, had given him a delicious cool drink of water and a piece of Scotch cake. He had prattled to the children of the long-ago days when Master Antinous's mamma was just such another little person as he was now, and used to come and pay him and his old lady a visit and eat cake just as he was doing.

A few days later Malcolm, coming with Antinous to the usual meeting-place under the beeches, found no one there. She went on to her father's cottage to ascertain the cause. She found her sister and mother in great distress. The little child was ill, and getting worse hour by hour. He complained of his throat, and was evidently suffering greatly. The doctor arrived presently and pronounced it a case of diphtheria. Malcolm,

when she heard it, gave a groan of horror.
She felt a dire presentiment of evil; she
knew that judgment was about to fall. She
locked herself in her room, fell on her knees,
prayed passionately, wildly, despairingly, that
it might fall on her, not on an innocent victim. But what avail the prayers of guilty
souls, even to assuage their own apprehensions? What avails the sacrifice when the
sacrificer's hand is stained with guilt? Malcolm, even while she prayed, felt a conviction
that Heaven was deaf, and that her prayer
would not be granted. Two days later she
learnt that her sister's child was dead. Presently Antinous began to sicken. Malcolm's
heart stood still with horror. She caught
the child to her arms in a paroxysm of grief
and terror. 'My God,' she cried, 'spare
him, spare him! Strike me! Punish me as
I deserve, but not the child! Anything but
that!'

CHAPTER XLVII

A CONFESSION

'*Mac.* Cure her of that.
Canst thou not minister to a mind diseas'd,
Pluck from the memory a rooted sorrow,
Raze out the written troubles of the brain
And with some sweet oblivious antidote
Cleanse the stuff'd bosom of the perilous stuff
Which weighs upon the heart?'

DESPITE Malcolm's prayers—despite assiduous nursing—despite the famous specialist who arrived, next morning, with Mrs. Heriot, Antinous grew steadily worse. Isabella, who had never had a real sorrow before, was beside herself with terror, fury, despair. 'Those,' says George Eliot, 'who have been indulged by fortune, and have always thought of calamity as what happens to others, feel a

blind, incredulous rage at the reversal of their
lot, and half believe that their wild cries will
alter the course of the storm.' Mrs. Heriot's
cries were wild and fierce. She turned on
Malcolm like a wild animal, the savage
mother who sees her offspring torn from her.
There was no question as to where and how
the malady had been caught. Malcolm had
received positive orders to take the child to
no cottage. She had chosen to disobey, the
child was dying in consequence. 'You are
his murderess, his murderess!' Mrs. Heriot
cried in her despair.

'Murderess!' cried Malcolm; 'you know
well that I would die to save him. I would
give my soul for him.'

'You have killed him!' burst out Mrs.
Heriot. 'His blood is on your head: you
have killed him. It will kill me. Die for
him, did you say? You sacrificed him to
your own amusement; you broke your word
to me. You have killed him.'

Malcolm's ashy lips trembled, but could fashion no reply. Her mistress's words fell like lashes on the shuddering flesh. She sat looking at her in a silent agony.

'Do not look at me like that,' cried Mrs. Heriot; 'you have an evil eye. What are you thinking?'

'I am thinking,' said the other, 'of something I have felt all the morning. I could not be sure that it was not fancy. But it was no fancy. I have not nursed Antinous for nothing. I have diphtheria myself. I am certain of it. I knew all along that I should catch it. Now, perhaps, you will forgive me.'

Isabella Heriot instinctively drew back; but there was no forgiveness, no pity in her tones. 'You shall nurse him no longer; you are his murderess!'

'Murderess!' cried the other, half frantic; 'you little know what I have done for him, for you! Take care what you drive me to!'

'Do not rave like a mad woman,' said her
mistress. 'Stay where you are. The doctor
will come to you.'

The doctor pronounced Malcolm's ill-
ness to be unquestionably diphtheria. It
was a serious case; her weak health, her
low vitality, her despondent mood, made
her a bad subject. She was ill equipped
for a life-struggle. Malcolm watched the
doctor's grave face. She gave a groan of
horror.

'Ah!' she cried, 'I knew it. I shall die!
I dare not! I will not! God help me! He is
punishing me for my sin, my grievous sin.
It has been my torture ever since. Now He
has stricken the child, and stricken me! It
was for the child's sake that I did it, and it
has been in vain. I must repent before I
die. May God forgive me!'

'Do not alarm yourself,' said the doctor,
taking a mental note of the extreme nervous-
ness of his patient, 'and show a little forti-

tude. If you wish to recover, that is the way to do it. You are in God's hand, remember.'

Malcolm gave a shudder.

'I remember it,' she said, 'only too well. There is no comfort to me in that.'

The next day Antinous was sinking fast. Mrs. Malcolm grew seriously worse. The doctor came from the bedside, where Antinous now lay almost *in extremis*. He found the sick woman in an agony of terror.

'Am I worse?' she demanded with passionate eagerness. 'Can I not recover? I am a strong woman. I never ailed before; my family is a long-lived one. Surely you can save me! For the love of God, save me, save me!'

'These cases are always dangerous,' said the doctor; 'but you must really keep calm. Have you anything on your mind?'

'Yes,' said Malcolm; 'a great sin is on

my mind. It is crushing me. I am a sinful
woman, and dying in my sin. Save me,
save me at any cost. I do not mind pain.
Is there nothing I can undergo?'

'I will send the clergyman to you, if you
please,' said the doctor. 'Perhaps he will
calm you. I can do no more for you.'

'I wish to tell you,' said the woman.
'Look, please, in my box; at the bottom
you will find a sheet of paper. It is Lady
Heriot's last codicil. I signed it, and my
sister Maggie signed it. She is here now,
and can tell you all. I have concealed it till
now. I have been guilty; but my guilt was
not to benefit myself.'

The doctor read the paper: 'I revoke the
codicil which I was constrained to sign this
afternoon. Let my will stand.'

'Those are the words,' said Malcolm;
'she bade me write them. I was nursing
her that night. She could not sleep. She
kept talking to herself. "I will not do it,"

she said. "Adrian wants it sorely. Antinous will be rich enough. Isabella forced
me." At last she bade me bring paper and
write to her dictation, then to call my sister,
who was sleeping in the next room. Then
we both saw her sign, and signed ourselves.
She put it under the pillow. After her
seizure the pillow was displaced, the paper
slipped to the floor. I picked it up. No
one had seen it. I knew that it meant ruin
to Antinous. It has been in my box ever
since. Maggie is here, and will tell you.
May God forgive me!'

'I must tell Mr. Heriot, of course,' said
the doctor.

'He must be told,' said the dying woman
with a groan.

'Shall I give him the paper?'

'Never!' cried Malcolm; 'give it to no
one but Sir Adrian.'

Maggie put her sister's story beyond
dispute. She remembered the occurrence,

recognised the paper and the signatures. She had not been aware of its importance, and had never thought of it till now; but her recollection was distinct. That evening little Antinous died.

CHAPTER XLVIII

EVENING LIGHTS

'Deus nobis hæc otia fecit.'

NOTHING in all the changes which Malcolm's disclosures had brought about in his position and prospects gave Sir Adrian more heart-felt satisfaction than the way in which his brother Valentine behaved. The two brothers had always at heart been longing for reconciliation. Each really loved the other. Both had grieved under the estrange-ment. Valentine had smarted under the stern sentence which banished him from the home, which, as years went on and the world's ambitions lost something of their attractiveness, was, he found, dearer to him than most things in life. In ordinary circumstances Sir Adrian might have found it hard to forgive, Valentine to accept forgiveness; but now a tragic sorrow bent both hearts in submission and linked them in sympathy.

Sir Adrian, standing over little Antinous's coffin, and watching his brother's haggard look of grief, could only seize his hand and seal an unspoken treaty of forgiveness. All was forgotten but the calamity which had shipwrecked the happiness, the hopes of one of them, and had turned the schemes, the labours, the ambitions of life to a hollow mockery, a ghastly comment on the vanity of human wishes. In that little coffin lay the object of all Valentine's busy life, his eager contrivance, his restless energy. For him he had toiled, for him he had plotted, for him he had sacrificed things once dear to him, which only so transcendent a sacrifice could claim. He had silenced conscience;

he had tampered with honour; he had for-
feited his friends' esteem, his brother's love.
Now all was over. Nothing remained to
wish, to hope, to labour for. Valentine
spoke to Sir Adrian with perfect frankness
about the money. 'It would all have been
Jack's one day,' he said, 'for, of course, as
matters stand, I should have left all to him;
to whom should I leave it? But I am glad
that this part of it is yours at once, Adrian.
I give you my honour I am glad to be rid of
it: it weighed on my soul. I have never
been happy since I got it. It has been a
curse to me. It has brought me a curse.
Now that it is gone, I may hope to be forgiven. You forgive me, at any rate?'

'And you must forgive me,' said Sir
Adrian, in the kind frank tones which
Valentine remembered as closing many a
boyish quarrel; 'I need forgiveness, God
knows. I have been wrong, very wrong.
I know it. I confess it humbly. I have

nursed my rage and thought about you like a brute. Forgive me, Valentine. Pray God forgive us both. I am thankful to be friends again. Dear brother, to my heart's core I sorrow for your loss.'

One other scene, a farewell scene, before the cares, joys, and sorrows of the Heriots fade from us into the gloom. A year has passed, and it is summer again, and Jack and Olivia—by this time wearing the dignities of an experienced married pair—have left their quarters in the Museum for a holiday at Jack's old home. Dr. Crucible has arrived for a Sunday in the country. The sacred rites of five-o'clock tea are in course of celebration under the great cedar on the lawn.

A year of prosperity had done wonders for Sir Adrian and his wife. Sir Adrian stood upright again, as a man should who has paid off his mortgages, owes no one a shilling, and is rich enough not to care if a

farm or two more or less remains unlet.
Lady Eugenia, relieved from her husband's
anxieties and Jack's love troubles, and re-
joicing in a daughter-in-law whom she found
every day more congenial to her taste, had
blossomed into a serenity and good-nature
which proved how heavily her former cares
had weighed upon her spirits. Olivia makes
a perfect daughter of the house. She has
now gone to summon Dr. Crucible from the
library, where he had been suspiciously quiet
for the last hour and a half. The two are
coming, arm in arm, across the lawn to join
the rest. 'A siesta?' said Sir Adrian; 'we
were obliged to disturb you; Olivia wants to
give you a cup of tea.'

'Base insinuation,' cried the doctor, showing a volume which he was holding in his
hand; 'I have been too well employed.
There is excellent good reading in the library.
I lighted on a volume of Emerson. What
do you think of this piece of philosophy?'

And then the doctor read—

' " Meanwhile life wears on and ministers to you, no
doubt, as to me, its undying and grand lessons, its un-
containable, endless poetry, its short dry prose of
scepticism, its veins of cold air in the evening woods,
quickly swallowed by the wide warmth of June, its steady
correction of the rashness and short sight of youthful
judgment, and its pure repairs of all the rents and
seeming ruin it operates in what it gave : although we
love the first gift so well that we cling to the ruin and
think we will be cold to the new if the new shall come.
But the new steals on us, like a star, which rises behind
our back as we walk, and we are borrowing gladly its
light before we know the benefactor.   So be it with you,
with me, with all." '

' I join in that prayer,' said Sir Adrian.
' My good star rose late, but it lends a kindly
light, and is leading me by pleasant paths.
May it shine upon us all.'

THE END

Printed by R. & R. CLARK, *Edinburgh.*